"**I** know you're up to something, Mac. May I call you Mac?"

"What?"

"You heard me."

Dr. George didn't say anything else, letting his last few sentences sink in. I sat there and let them. And I didn't like it. I didn't like those words a single bit.

"I'm going to find out what's going on. I'll be watching you closely. I don't tolerate funny *business* in my school, as I said. Maybe you kids got to do whatever you wanted before, but now that I'm here, all of that will change. This school is more important than any of you realize, and nothing is going to get in the way of me cleaning it up, understand?"

I wasn't sure if he'd emphasized the word "business" on purpose or if my mind was just playing tricks on me. The effect was the same, regardless. My business was in danger from the worse source possible: the Administration. I could handle rival businesses, tough customers, rats, snitches, and general troublemakers. But the one thing I couldn't have against me was the Administration. As dumb as the suits usually were, they still held the power to shut me down for good.

ALSO BY
Chris Rylander

The Fourth Stall
The Fourth Stall Part III

Chris Rylander

The Fourth Stall

PART II

WALDEN POND PRESS
An Imprint of HarperCollinsPublishers

Walden Pond Press is an imprint of HarperCollins Publishers.
Walden Pond Press and the skipping stone logo are trademarks and
registered trademarks of Walden Media, LLC.

The Fourth Stall Part II
Copyright © 2012 by Chris Rylander
address HarperCollins Children's Books, a division of HarperCollins
Publishers, 10 East 53rd Street, New York, NY 10022.
www.harpercollinschildrens.com

Library of Congress Cataloging-in-Publication Data
Rylander, Chris.
    The fourth stall. Part II / Chris Rylander. — 1st ed.
        p.   cm.
    Summary: Sixth graders Mac and Vince, who operate an advice
and assistance service for fellow students, face new dangers when a
strict administrator is hired to clean up the school and a strange and
dangerous girl asks for their help to have a teacher fired.
    ISBN 978-0-06-199631-3
    [1. Business enterprises—Fiction.   2. Schools—Fiction.]   I. Title.
PZ7.R98147Fp   2012   2011022935
[Fic]—dc23   CIP
                                                                 AC

            12 13 14 15 16   LP/BR   10 9 8 7 6 5 4 3 2 1
                                   ❖
                    First paperback edition, 2013

For Amanda, always

Tuesday—The Fourth Stall

I knew she would be trouble from the moment I saw her.

Perhaps because she was soaking wet from the rain even though an umbrella stuck out from her backpack or maybe simply because she was a girl—an especially dangerous-looking girl at that. In grade school they say girls are more dangerous than shotguns.

I'd helped out plenty of girls with problems before. That's what I do. If there's a kid in this school who needs help, they come to see me in my office in the fourth stall from the high window in the East Wing boys' bathroom. And plenty of those kids over the years had been girls.

But this girl was different than most girls. She was only an eighth grader, but she seemed even older. There was something almost predatory about her, like a rattlesnake sat across from me and not a girl. And I felt like a small white mouse or whatever it is that rattlesnakes eat.

I cleared my throat as she sat there staring at me. Her eyes were bright green and glowed like the neon signs you see in pawnshop windows. Her hair was dark, not quite black but dark enough to remind me what my teacher had said once about how objects that are black absorb all frequencies of light so that none can be seen, as if they want to keep all color to themselves. The girl's hair hung past her shoulders in intentional tangles that looked like they could eat a kid alive. She was dressed as if she cared just enough to make it look like she didn't care, and I kind of liked that about her.

"So what can I do for you?" I asked.

She shook her wet hair and little droplets of cold water splashed across my desk and on my face. She stopped and looked at me, her thin, dark eyebrows forming two perfect, high arches.

I wiped off my face with my sleeve.

"Oh, uh, right," I said. "Hey, Vince, can we get a towel or something in here?"

After an uncomfortable silence during which the dark-haired girl kept staring at me, Vince, my right-hand man, financial manager, best friend, and overall good guy, came into the stall with a bunch of brown paper towels clutched in his hand.

"Will these do, Mac?"

I looked at the paper towels. They were the same cheap stuff found in every school from here to Canada and back. They're stiff and dry, and you're more likely to rub your skin raw right down to the bone than you are to dry yourself.

"That's all we got?"

Vince shrugged.

"They'll be fine," the dark-haired girl said as she snatched the towels from Vince.

Vince stood there looking like a sheep about to get sheared naked.

"Okay, we're good," I said to him.

He snapped out of it and left the stall to take up his post just inside the bathroom door.

I watched the dark-haired girl try to dry her hair with the mass of brown paper towels. More water fell onto her shoulders and my desk than was actually soaked up by the brown stuff.

"I'm Mac, by the way," I said.

"I know."

"Oh, right. Okay, what's your name?"

"Are you trying to help me or ask me out?" she asked.

I felt my face grow hot, and I was sure it was glowing

red right then, despite the fact that I always asked my customers for their names. It's for bookkeeping—I run a pretty tight ship. Normally I operate much more smoothly than this. It's my office, my business; I run the show. But this girl was making me feel like it was my first day of kindergarten.

Then she laughed. But it sounded even worse than the icy silence of a few moments before. It sounded like the blurring rattle of an about-to-strike rattlesnake.

"I'm just messing with you, Mac."

I tried to laugh back.

"Anyways, the reason I'm here is because I heard you might be able to help me."

I nodded.

"Okay, well, the problem is this jerk Bryce who goes to Oaks Crossing private school over in Riverdale. I went out with him for a while and then he . . . ugh. Well, he's just a whiny loser!" The dark-haired girl slammed her fist on my desk. My pen rattled and dropped to the floor.

I leaned over to pick it up, more than a little frightened at how quickly she'd gone from wet and angry to laughing and scary to angry and, well, angry.

"Okay, so Bryce is like your boyfriend or something, then?" I said as I faced her again.

"No, weren't you listening? Why would I date a jerk like him?" she said.

"Oh yeah, well, I thought you said . . ."

"What *is* it with boys? Seriously? Do you all have, like, mental defects that prevent you from understanding simple sentences?"

I opened my mouth, but all I could do was shrug and shake my head.

"I *said* dat-*ed*, as in past tense. I broke up with the loser weeks ago."

"Oh," I said.

She looked at me, her mouth open. Her neon eyes glared, and I almost had to shield my face. If there had still been a toilet in the fourth stall from the high window, I'd have been trying desperately to flush myself down it right then.

"Are you *slow*?" she asked. She said it calmly. Sincerely. As if she already knew the answer was yes and was now just afraid she was going to hurt my feelings.

"No, of course not. So you, what, need me to get back at Bryce for you or something?"

She sighed.

"Why would I need that? *I* broke up with *him*. Remember?"

It felt like this girl was twisting my brain into a pretzel. I remembered that she'd said that, but I'd just spaced out. She had me so mixed up I could barely remember my own name.

"Oh yeah—yes. What do you need help with, then? Do you need protection from him?" I asked as professionally as I could. But I sure hoped that wasn't the case. The last kid that had come in here looking for protection had ended up almost destroying my whole business. But that's another story.

"What? From that moron? No. He's too stupid to pose any kind of threat to anybody but himself. It's his dad who's the real problem."

I almost asked her why she hadn't just said that to begin with, but I thought better of it. After all, if you come across a rattlesnake in a field, the dumbest thing to do would be to poke it with a stick. So I just nodded instead.

"I think his dad is out to get me," she said.

As she spoke, she fiddled with the corner of my Books, which I use to track my customers and their different problems. I watched as she folded the corner of a sheet back and forth, creasing it. I wanted to stop her because I like to keep nice, neat Books, but then I realized that I was afraid to say something. Even after everything I'd faced over the years, I was afraid of an unarmed girl. That is if you could ever really call *any* girl "unarmed" . . . unless of course she was a girl who really didn't have any arms, in which case you'd probably feel too bad for her to be afraid anyway.

Meanwhile she just kept on folding, back and forth, back and forth. The page tore a little and I winced as if she'd broken my pinkie.

"Are you even listening to me?" she asked.

I realized that I'd been staring vacantly at her pale fingers as they desecrated my Books, and I wasn't really paying attention to what she'd been saying. I opened my mouth and closed it a few times.

"You know what? Forget it." She started to gather her things and get up.

I really should have just let her go. She scared me. She made my head feel like a nut clamped firmly inside a squirrel's jaw. But my business doesn't work like that. If you have a problem, *I am going to solve it*. So I stopped her.

"Wait," I said. "I'm sorry. I can help you, I promise."

She sat back down and closed her left eye. She examined me closely with her one open eye. After a moment she was looking at me with two again.

"Okay, what I was saying is that Bryce's dad has been a real jerk to me in class. I think that Bryce went bawling to his daddy after I dumped him like the loser that he is, and now his dad is out to fail me and make sure that I don't ever get to high school. Or maybe worse . . . maybe he's trying to get me expelled. He yells at me in class a lot, he erases my correct answers on tests and writes in wrong ones so I fail, and he always gives me detention for nothing at all."

I hadn't heard the part about Bryce's dad working at our school, but I wasn't going to ask her to clarify again, because if I did, I was sure she'd dig her venom-filled fangs into me and that'd be it.

"Which teacher is his dad?"

"Mr. Kjelson."

"Mr. Kjelson, the new guy?"

"Do you know another Mr. Kjelson?"

"Right. Sorry."

Now I was more confused than ever. Mr. Kjelson had just started working at our school a few months ago after one of the older seventh-grade science teachers, Mrs. Beck, mysteriously vanished one day. Well, I'm sure *somebody* knew what had happened to her, but nobody I knew did. She was there one day and the next she was gone. I heard from a few kids in her classes that she hadn't even come back to get the stuff on her desk, like pictures of her family and all of that.

Anyways, at first I didn't pay much attention to Mr. K. (that's what all the kids call him since his name is like a phonics test of bravery, complete with a man-eating, double-consonant-breathing dragon right at the start). But then I found out he was going to be the new middle school baseball coach this year. And, well, that definitely caught my interest since Vince and I had always been planning to try out for the middle school team as sixth graders ever since we were kindergartners.

It was pretty tough to make the team as a sixth grader, but if anybody could do it, it'd be Vince. He is, without question, the best pitcher I've ever caught. Well, okay, so he's also the only pitcher I've ever caught, but last summer in pony baseball, which is organized through the local recreation center, he'd struck out thirteen batters in six innings in the only game our idiotic coach, Colton, let him start. Colton was this high school kid who only pretended to like sports to impress girls and who the rec center assigned to our team. And he had a little brother named Chase who he let pitch every game despite the fact that Chase was like the Joe Blanton of summer little league: good on paper but horrible in an actual game. That was part of why we were so eager to make the school team this year rather than play in the rec league: to get away from idiot teenage coaches like Colton.

In fact, the first day of tryouts for pitchers and catchers was after school that day in the gymnasium, since it was still too cold to have practice outside. I'd heard some good things about Mr. Kjelson, both as a coach and teacher. Supposedly some kid who played against the team he'd coached last year said that Mr. Kjelson loved small ball, and anybody who loves small ball clearly knows baseball. Also, even after just part of a year as a teacher, the rumor already was that he was the best science teacher the school had ever had. Supposedly when he taught class, he explained things by comparing all the boring science stuff to funny, weird, and cool stuff like using Mr. T's haircut when explaining how a disease worked, turning the periodic table into a rap song, and using Harry Potter characters to explain our internal organs.

So long story short, what this girl was telling me right now didn't really add up.

"Mr. Kjelson does all of that? Are you sure?"

She gave me a look that could have melted gold. "You think I don't even know who my own teachers are? Yeah, of course I'm sure!"

"Oh, right, sorry. I just, it's just that that's not really matching up with what I've heard about the guy, that's all," I said.

"Well, do you always believe everything you hear around here? Because if so, then I'm probably wasting my time," she said, starting to get up again.

"No, wait," I said. "I mean, I actually do have pretty good sources. But I suppose they have been wrong before."

She looked at me and didn't say anything else. I

looked back, getting the bad feeling that she was waiting for me to say more. But for whatever reason I didn't know what to do next, which was a first for me—like I said, I run a pretty tight business.

When I didn't say anything after a few more seconds, she rolled her eyes.

"So can you help me or not?" the dark-haired girl demanded.

I nodded and folded my hands in front of me. "You just want me to get Kjelson off your back? Yeah, I think we can work something out, provided he's as corrupt as you say he is."

She started giggling, going from anger to laughter faster than I could have thought possible. She rocked back in her chair and slapped the desk with her open palm. "You. Are. So. Cute."

My face burned even though I figured my brain might explode at any moment because I was so confused. I couldn't figure why she was laughing at me. Was it because I was trying to be professional? This is a respectable business, and I treat it like one; everybody knows that. What was it with this girl?

"I'm sorry, I'm sorry," she said as she managed to stifle the last of her giggles.

"So, uh, can I get your name for my Books?" I asked, picking up my pen.

She snorted one final guffaw. "Trixie Von Parkway."

Just to be clear, I didn't believe that for a second. But that was okay; I'd had plenty of kids give me false names over the years. I could get her real name if I really needed it. It's not difficult to get information when you've got guys like Tyrell Alishouse on your payroll. He's about the best spy that ever existed. He could probably find Jimmy Hoffa in under an hour if I put him on the case.

"Is that it, then? You'll just take care of it?" she asked.

"Yeah, well, um, there's also the matter of, uh, payment," I said, coughing at the end of the sentence like I'd seen my dad do once while he negotiated the purchase of a new car. He talked them down to the sticker price, which he said was a steal. I'd never been so afraid to go over my payment terms before. I didn't like what this girl was doing to me; I had a reputation to uphold.

"Oh, right. How much will it be?" she asked.

"Well, dealing with teachers is normally a pretty costly service, due to the risk involved, but I can probably cut you a break. How does twenty-five dollars sound?"

"I'll give you ten."

"Fifteen," I countered.

"Eight," she said.

I stopped and looked at her. She grinned at me. Most customers would have gotten the boot right then and there for that kind of stunt. But most customers didn't remind me of a seventeen-foot rattler with nine-inch fangs.

"Hey, *you* came to *me* for help, remember?"

She laughed. "Okay, fifteen. But only because I like you, Mac."

Could have fooled me.

"Payment is usually due up front," I said.

"I'll pay you when I'm sure Kjelson is off my back. It was nice doing business." She held out her hand.

When I reached out and shook it, I expected her fingers to be sticky and slimy, for some reason, but they were just cold. Freezing, actually. After she left, I cupped my hands and blew into them, trying to shake off the fact that I'd just been manhandled like a slab of ground beef about to become a dozen fried hamburgers.

Chapter 2

Tuesday—The Fourth Stall

We didn't really even have time to start thinking about how to solve Trixie's problem that day because the customers just didn't stop showing up. It was one of the busiest days we've ever had in the history of our business. At lunch that Tuesday I had two more customers show up with pretty major problems.

The first was this kid Jonah. He was a seventh grader and was known around school for being a real health freak, the kind of grade-A nut job who liked to go on "fun runs." He'd made the school varsity cross-country team that year as a sixth grader, which was downright unheard of. Personally I'd rather take a honey bath followed by a flesh-eating-ant shower than spend my

Saturdays running eighty-eight miles in six hours or whatever other psychotic kind of stuff happened at cross-country meets, but just the same he became the team's star runner, and our school had been getting a lot of attention lately around the county because we always seemed to be the best at every sport and the local private high schools were always trying to recruit us away from the district public schools.

Anyway, Jonah showed up in my office that day at lunch wearing a gray T-shirt and running shorts that were borderline vulgar, they were so short, and were also a bad choice given that it was still below forty degrees outside and would be for the next few months. Seriously, runners are insane.

After Vince showed him in, Jonah jogged in place across from my desk in my cramped office while trying not to kick the fourth stall's door behind him.

"You can have a seat," I said, finding his high steps particularly distracting and grotesque.

"Nah, I'm good," he said, picking up the pace of his steps.

I sighed, but I don't think he heard me, which was probably good since that was pretty unprofessional of me. "Okay, what can I help you with, Jonah?"

He didn't answer because he was holding two fingers against his neck with his left hand while looking at a watch on his right wrist. He kept jogging in place and then said, "Shoot, only ninety-one," and then picked up the pace even more.

This was going to get old in a hurry.

"Look, Jonah," I said, "I'm going to need you to sit down if you want my help."

He looked at me as if he'd forgotten I was there. He kept jogging in place, and for a second I thought he might just keep doing that until I'd have to call in Joe to forcibly remove him. But Jonah nodded and then sat in the plastic chair across from me.

"Okay, thanks," I said. "Now, how can I help you?"

"Well, I'm here about the school lunches," he said as his knees started bouncing up and down.

Man, this kid was restless. He was basically running in place while seated. I didn't know if he had one of those letter diseases that parents were always freaking out about, like ADD or DUD or whatever, or if he was just that obsessed with running, but either way he was driving me crazy.

"Lunch? Yeah, what about it?" I asked while calmly putting my Books inside the desk and out of harm's way.

"Haven't you noticed how bad the meal options are lately?"

I actually hadn't noticed anything different about the school lunches at all, since I brought my own lunch most days and spent every lunch period in here seeing customers. But, I mean, who was this kid kidding? Everybody knows that school lunch is awful. It's, like, common knowledge. It's one of those things you're just born knowing, like how cats know how to catch mice even if they didn't ever have their mom around. It's instinct for kids to avoid school lunch. At the very least hadn't Jonah ever seen any of those lame shows on Nickelodeon or read any books about kids in school?

"Lately?" I said. "I mean, they've always been terrible, based on what kids have told me. And like I told all of them, there's not much I can do about that. . . . I mean, I can get you McDonalds or something for lunch on certain occasions or even regularly if you pay the right price, but getting the lunch ladies to cook even halfway decent food is a lost cause. It would be like asking me to get them to cancel school forever so we could all go live in some magical land where there are no adults except for a ship full of pirates and a tiny fairy who glows. You know?"

"No, no, no," Jonah said, waving his hands. With his feet bouncing even faster and his arms waving about, he looked certifiably crazy. If I'd had a Taser right then, I might have used it on him. For his own safety. "Not bad as in 'they taste bad.' I meant how bad they are for you. They've been incredibly unhealthy lately, like mucho trans-fat and simple-carb type unhealthy."

He said that last part while nodding with bugged-out eyes as if those words were supposed to say everything I needed to know. But the fact was I didn't have a clue what he was talking about. So I just nodded calmly, hoping that he'd take that as a sign to go on. Or leave.

"I mean," he continued, "yesterday for lunch they served us deep-fried bacon and frosted pancakes with double-berry syrup, and last week it was fried chicken with sides of fried chicken skin and double-fried French fries and chicken-fried steak with fried mashed-potato cakes and double-cream gravy. Basically, if a dish contains the word 'double,' 'gravy,' or 'fried,' then it's been on the menu during the past few weeks!"

I opened my mouth to ask him what the big deal was, since I thought all that stuff sounded really good. In fact, I was starting to think I might need to try this new school lunch. But he started screaming before I could say anything.

"Do you know how many calories are in that stuff? I mean, it's like a ton of calories! Or how much saturated fat? How much LDL cholesterol?" He was on his feet again now, jogging in place. That seemed to be the only thing holding Jonah together right then so I allowed it.

I tried not to laugh because my mom and her friends were always going on and on about those evil calories and it just sounded so strange coming from a seventh grader. He didn't seem much like my mom and those weird ladies she hung out with who wore tracksuits all the time and sat around the kitchen talking about calories and exercises while eating all of the double chocolate chip cookies they'd just baked.

"Okay, Jonah," I said, "we'll help you, but you've got to calm down."

The truth was I wasn't too sure I wanted to solve this problem. If these lunches were as good as they sounded and then I somehow fixed the "problem" and the student body found out it was me . . . well, then I'd be as good as dead. Or worse yet, they'd probably douse me in breading and double fry me and then take turns dunking me in ranch dressing and taking bites. Okay, that's pretty gross, but it's also probably pretty accurate. But I had to help Jonah, regardless. I mean, look at this kid; he clearly wasn't going to survive this if I didn't figure out what was going on. And, well, a whole bunch of disappointed kids is still better than a bunch of happy, gorging kids and one calorie-exploded cross-country runner. Plus, he had a point—it was pretty strange for the school to be serving that kind of food.

"Do you know how many calories, Mac? Do you?" he yelled again.

"We'll help you, Jonah. Just calm down," I said again.

He didn't seem to hear me; he just kept on rambling and running in place. "I mean, this isn't a recommended diet. No, not at all. We're supposed to have a well-balanced meal consisting of lean proteins and vitamin-packed green vegetables and a few complex carbohydrates, like plain brown rice or whole-grain bread. But this . . . oh, this is just not ideal, not at all. I mean, the calories alone, not to mention the trans-fats and simple carbohydrates . . . and . . . and the calories!"

"Vince?" I called out.

"Yeah, Mac?" I heard him say, and from the way he said it, I knew he was laughing so hard out there that it was likely he was rolling on the floor.

"Tell Joe we need a peaceful extraction," I said.

"I'm on it!" Vince said through a loud laugh.

Jonah didn't seem to notice; he was still just jogging in place and muttering about calories over and over again. Then he seemed to be counting silently for a bit before saying to nobody in particular, "That must be like three thousand calories!"

Joe entered and grabbed Jonah's shoulders, but not in a rough way, and led him out of the stall and then out of the office. Every once in a while we had to extract kids, usually for my protection, but this time it was for Jonah's own protection. In that cramped stall he was pretty likely to have hurt himself had he kept going on and on like that. I gave Vince, who was still laughing, a look and then went back to my office to make a note to be sure to discuss payment terms with Jonah sometime the following day.

Jonah's problem was pretty typical, actually. Kids seemed to have pretty big problems with the school lately. The usual customer needed his homework done for him, or test answers, or something I could fix easily. But lately they'd been asking for some pretty major fixes, like getting a teacher fired and changing an entire school's lunch menu. That said, I wasn't complaining, because this would probably end well for us—very well, actually. The more difficult a problem is, the more money I get to charge. Which is why I was actually kind of happy when another kid showed up with a major problem later that lunch period.

Tony Adrian walked into the office looking like he was trying to float inside. I mean, he shuffled his feet very close together, and his steps were so light, it looked like they were barely touching the ground. I saw that he had his backpack with him, and I looked at Vince, who was standing just outside the fourth stall.

He nodded that it was okay. Normally we didn't allow kids to bring stuff inside my office, but after a search and if they had a reason, we sometimes allowed it. I wasn't sure what Adrian's reasoning was, but if Vince had okayed the backpack, then I wasn't going to say anything. I trusted Vince more than I trusted myself sometimes.

"Have a seat," I said to Tony, who was still standing there as Vince closed the stall door.

Tony dug inside his backpack and removed a small plastic container. I tensed as he reached inside, but then all he took out was a little white disposable towel, the kind that restaurants put on the plate when you order barbecue ribs or buffalo wings. You know, the towels soaked in so many cleaning chemicals that they smell like they could burn your skin right off your hands.

Tony wiped down the plastic chair with the towel and then sat down. I gave him a look and he shrugged sheepishly.

"So what can I help you with?"

"Well, it's something I've been finding in my locker lately—" He put his hand to his mouth as if he was going to puke, then he swallowed hard and continued. "I like to keep my stuff pretty clean, you see, and the past few days I've been finding droppings in my locker."

He shuddered at the end of his sentence and then breathed hard, as if just saying that had taken as much energy as running a lap.

"Droppings?"

"Yes . . . feces of some kind. I think probably from a

mouse, but it's hard to say. I can . . . barely look at it." His sentences were choppy because he had to keep putting his hand to his mouth and swallowing, as if every word carried the danger of coming out covered in Tony's breakfast.

"Rat poop in your locker, eh?" I said as if this was something that happened all the time. It wasn't.

He nodded, seeming relieved to be using wordless gestures.

"So you just want me to help you clean it up?" I asked. "You don't want to touch it, I'm assuming?"

It wasn't hard to see that this kid was a neat freak of epic proportions. I thought my mom was bad, but this kid would probably make her look like the Ron Santo of cleaning, which is pretty good, but just not good enough for the Hall of Fame, for some reason.

"Yeah, help me clean it, but also maybe try to find out where it's coming from? And get it to stop? It's been kind of piling . . . up." He struggled to get out the last few words, and I slid back from the desk as far as I could, sure that this was it, that he was going to lose it.

But he controlled himself, probably because the sight of the mess he'd have made would have instantly caused him to combust into a ball of fire.

"Okay, I'm sure we can figure something out," I said. "But poop duty isn't exactly our favorite thing to do, right, so it'll probably cost you about four bucks every time we need to clean your locker. And then a little more to solve the problem entirely, maybe like eleven dollars. How does that sound? Unless you'd rather pay with a favor?"

"Can I think about it?" he asked. "I mean, I can pay you now for the cleaning, but for the rest can I think about the money or favor part?"

"That sounds fair," I said.

He nodded and dug inside his backpack. Well, he didn't so much as dig as he carefully extracted a small Tupperware container as if it contained highly unstable radioactive uranium. It did not contain explosives, though, but instead several neatly folded and impeccably clean plastic sandwich bags. Inside each bag was a different type of money. One bag had all pennies and one had dollar bills, etc.

He carefully opened the bag with one dollar bills like he was performing a complicated and risky brain surgery. He reached inside and took out four of the crispest one-dollar bills I'd ever seen. They were so straight and neat and crispy that I bet they would have crunched like Pringles if I decided to take a bite out of one.

He handed me the money and then gathered his things. I filed away the money and made some notes in my Books.

"It was good doing business," I said with my hand outstretched.

He looked at my hand as if it were a giant ball of boogers or something even more disgusting. I wasn't sure if I should be offended. I mean, okay, I wasn't like Mr. Clean over here, but I wasn't exactly like Dirty Mike, the kid who hadn't showered in four years, seven months, and fourteen days—yes, he actually kept track; he claimed he was trying to beat a world record of some sort, though I don't know why anyone would ever keep a record book for who's the dirtiest, grossest person on earth.

But then Tony did shake my hand. Afterward, he immediately took out one of his little towels and wiped off his hand. Instead of getting mad, though, I just grinned at him. I mean, what else was I going to do? This kid clearly had issues that only a professional could handle.

"We'll be sure to clean your locker by tomorrow morning. Just let me know if and when it needs to be cleaned again while we work on solving the problem permanently."

"Okay, thanks, Mac," he said while standing up and putting on his backpack.

He opened the stall door and left, and just before he walked out of my field of vision, I saw him pulling out another towel to wipe his hand. I shook my head and smirked at Vince, who was leaning against the wall across from the fourth stall. He grinned back. And then when the door closed and Tony was gone, we both burst out laughing.

We stayed pretty busy the rest of the day. No one else complained about lunches or rat poop or Mr. Kjelson, but we did get quite a few more kids with big school problems. A few kids even complained that bullies weren't getting punished as much as usual. Like Great White, this British kid who loved to fight. Usually when he was caught fighting, he got at least a few days of detention. But lately, according to two customers that day, all he got was one hour of detention, so he'd been picking fights even more than usual. Basically all of this just meant big money for us. As long as nothing crazy happened in the next few weeks, we were going to walk away from this month with record profits. Our Cubs World Series Game Fund would reach an all-time high soon.

Later that day, at the end of afternoon recess, Fred, Vince, Joe, and I held a quick meeting to discuss all of the business that had bombed us that day.

"Well, it's like my grandma always says, 'There ain't no can of—'" Vince said.

" 'Of soda that can dance as well as a lion with no toes?' " I finished for him.

"Hey, how did you know that?" Vince looked hurt.

"Because you've already used that one before."

Vince looked down at the tiles of the bathroom and furrowed his brow.

"Yeah, remember? It was right after Fred told us about how they had to dance in gym class last week," Joe said.

Vince looked up and smiled. "Oh yeah. Now I remember. Well, I guess that one is just versatile, right? I always said my grandma's a genius."

We laughed, more at the thought of Vince's grandma being a genius than anything else.

"That girl today seemed crazy, though, didn't she, Mac?" Fred asked.

He had heard our whole conversation, being that he sat in the stall next to my office and kept a detailed written record of each customer I saw.

"That's just how girls are. You'll see what I mean someday," Joe said.

"Right, like you would know," I said.

Joe shrugged.

"I don't know; I kind of liked her," Vince said.

We looked at him, ready for some sort of joke or something. Because he couldn't be serious. That girl was crazy. Even a little third grader like Fred could see that.

But Vince merely shrugged. "What? I like crazy people, remember?"

Fred and Joe laughed.

"Okay, whatever. None of this answers the big questions: is any of her story about Kjelson true? And if so, how should we deal with him?"

I'm not proud of it, but I'd taken down several teachers over the years, or at least gotten some customers around their problems somehow. But it was harder with new teachers. I didn't know much about them, and the janitor, who was usually my best source for dirt on teachers, wouldn't know much yet either. All of this could be beside the point, though. Trixie seemed a bit unstable, and what I'd heard about Mr. Kjelson made him sound like a stand-up guy. I would definitely need to look into things a little before diving in with my guns blazing. So to speak anyway—obviously I don't own any real guns.

"I don't know, Mac. You're the genius," Joe said.

"I'll think of something, I guess. Maybe Vince and I can get a better feel for the situation at baseball tryouts today. Then tomorrow we'll have to start investigating Jonah's lunchroom problem and Tony's, uh, poop issue."

Fred giggled, and Vince and I exchanged looks. Third graders. Have to love them.

"So any volunteers on that one?" I said.

They all looked at one another. Of course nobody wanted to volunteer for poop duty.

"Maybe we could outsource the cleaning?" Vince suggested.

"Outsource?" Joe said, sounding as confused as the rest of us probably were.

"Basically we can pay someone outside the business to clean Tony's locker. Like the Hutt. He probably showers in toilet water anyway."

"Gross," Fred said, and then giggled again in that way all third graders do at basically anything that involves poop or pee or vomit.

I agreed that was pretty gross, but Vince had made a good point. The Hutt was this bully who'd gotten his nickname because he was basically a big old slug like Jabba the Hutt from Star Wars. He'd probably do that locker job for cheap, maybe even for free if we let him keep the, uh, mess. That was a stretch, but this was the Hutt we're talking about.

"That's a great idea. Let's bring him in tomorrow," I said. "Then Vince and I can team up to take the mystery of how the poop is getting in his locker in the first place. It will be just like old times." It wasn't that often that Vince and I had to do fieldwork together anymore, but considering the amount of customers we'd had lately, it was pretty obvious we'd all have to pitch in quite a bit.

Vince's eyes lit up. "Can I even wear my old-timey hat like I used to?"

"What are you talking about?" Joe said.

"Don't ask," I said.

Vince had found this old hat at the secondhand store a long time ago. It was the kind that you see gangsters wearing in those old movies about Al Capone and tommy guns and stuff. Back in the early days of our business Vince used to wear it all the time, in spite of my protests—or maybe because of them.

"Oh, I almost forgot!" Vince said. "I've been thinking about this one all day. You ready, Mac?"

Joe and Fred groaned, and wandered out of the bathroom to go back to class since recess was ending soon.

"When aren't I ready?" I said after they left.

"Hey, just checking. I still haven't forgotten how you weaseled out of defeat a few months ago."

"Weaseled? Staples almost killed me!" I practically yelled, even though I wasn't really mad at all.

"All right, whatever. Here it is: before 2007 and 2008 when was the last time the Cubs went to the play-offs two years in a row?"

The Chicago Cubs were our favorite baseball team. Cubs baseball was like oxygen to us. No, really. We'd be a couple of pale blue corpses without it. We had this thing where we were always challenging each other with Cubs trivia.

"You're really asking that now?" I said, my voice not really shielding the hurt.

This was a painful time for us. The Cubs had been knocked out of the play-offs a few months ago. They'd made it further than they had in decades. It still hurt to think about how close they had come to a World Series. They haven't won a championship for over a hundred years, the longest drought in all of sports history. It was shocking that Vince could just bring up the play-offs like this.

"What? It's a fair question," he said.

"I know, I know. The answer is 1907 and 1908, the last time they won the World Series. Thanks a lot now, for jinxing them for next year, too."

"Whatever. They were doomed before I even said anything."

I smiled and nodded. "Yeah, they were, weren't they?"

That's the thing about the Cubs. They were so deeply cursed that they were jinx proof. They had a permanent jinx, and nothing anybody said or did would ever change that.

Chapter 3

Tuesday—The Olson Olson Theatre

The school held a surprise assembly shortly after recess ended. All of the students and teachers were called down to the Olson Olson Theatre, which was the name of the school's new, expensive theater. How it got such a ridiculous name is kind of a long story, so maybe I'll share it some other time.

Kids whispered among themselves as everybody found seats. Even some of the teachers looked curious. Unplanned all-school assemblies were unusual. And, to be honest, they made me a little nervous.

Principal Dickerson walked onto the stage after everyone was settled. He stepped up to the microphone and started talking. He didn't say good afternoon and make us answer him back; he didn't say hi; he didn't even smile. But then again Dickerson never did any of those things; he was a no-nonsense type of guy. "No-nonsense" is an expression I've heard my dad use before. I think it's like a polite way for adults to call people jerks.

"As some of you may be aware, the school has been having some discipline issues lately, as well as some other internal areas of concern. As a result, the school board has decided to bring in a vice principal for the indefinite future. He will primarily be in charge of handling all disciplinary issues and also will be investigating any and all other reported or suspected funny business. Also, I want to remind you all that . . ."

As Mr. Dickerson droned on about showing respect and remembering what we're all there to do and blah, blah, blah, I couldn't help but wonder where the heck the phrase "funny business" had come from. I mean, why did old people call bad acts "funny business"? Shouldn't they call it, like, "bad business" or "corrupt activities" or something more fitting? I snapped out of my wondering in time to catch the new vice principal's introduction.

". . . and so I'd like to welcome our new vice principal, Dr. George."

I think the student body was supposed to clap because I saw some teachers doing it, but basically nobody really did, so the few claps that were echoing around the room sounded especially lonely and unwelcoming. But I didn't care about that. All I cared about was trying to confirm if Dickerson had said what I just thought he had, that Dr. George was our new vice principal.

Dr. George was kind of famous in this area. He was known for being the toughest school principal around. He'd cleaned up some of the worst schools in the area. There were even articles in the local newspapers about him a year ago because he'd whipped into shape this one nearby high school that had been so unruly and horrible that people had started calling it the Failure Factory.

Dr. George wasn't a real doctor, like the kind you'd go to see if you were sick. Apparently you can become, like, another kind of doctor, too. I'm not sure exactly how that works, but all I know is that in my experience the fake doctors like Dr. George were usually a lot meaner, and thought they were the smartest people alive.

My fears were confirmed when our new VP walked up onto the stage. I recognized his stiff toupee from the pictures he'd had in the papers. His eyes bulged from his skull like analog sticks on a PlayStation controller. He and Dickerson shook hands and then George stepped to the podium.

"Well, thank you for the warm welcome," he said. He wasn't smiling. "We're going to have this school running smoothly very soon. Rest assured, anybody who wishes to prevent this from happening or insists on causing problems will be punished to the fullest extent of the school bylaws. From here forward funny business of any kind will not be tolerated.

"Additionally, we're going to be administering new state-government-funded and -monitored tests called the Standardized Minimum Aptitude Reviewer Tests, or SMARTs. These tests are an accurate barometer for student achievement and education quality, and I myself have personally worked with state officials and other school administrators within the state to help develop these tests to be effective, efficient, and consistent in their accuracy. They can measure this school's or any school's success in a quantifiable way, which is to say, in a way that can be scientifically measured. The quantification of the abstract is one of mankind's greatest achievements, and we expect to explore that further here.

"The SMARTs are only one small part of a new initiative that I will be working into your school this year in an attempt to clean this place up and make it a suitable institute of American education, suitable for American students. That is all; you are dismissed."

That was that. He was a man of few words, I guessed. Another no-nonsense guy, which basically meant that now we had two jerks running this place.

There were murmurs across the room as kids stood

up. Clearly some of them knew who Dr. George was, and they knew his reputation. Some didn't, but I had a feeling that we all would know him all too well soon enough. Other kids were murmuring about the SMARTs that Dr. George had talked about with so much pride on stage that you'd have thought the test was like his own flesh and blood—which knowing how dry Suits usually were, it was totally possible that Dr. George was made up of paper and documents and statistics as opposed to blood and bone and guts like the rest of us. But anyway, you know how kids are; they always overreact to those two words: "big test."

I wondered briefly if some of the "internal areas of concern" that Mr. Dickerson had mentioned were the very same problems that kids had been coming to me for lately. If so, then Dr. George's arrival was now a problem on two fronts: 1) He was a hawk for troublemakers and funny business, which were basically my bread and butter, how I made a living; and 2) He was potentially going to be working to solve the very same problems that I needed to solve myself to keep making money. Either way you shook it, I didn't like it. Not at all.

It was like putting Joe Blanton in the game to pinch-hit in the ninth inning with the bases loaded and down by three, which is to say that it was becoming a no-win situation because, for one, you'd never want a pitcher pinch-hitting, and two, it's Joe Blanton.

Ripping on Joe Blanton had become kind of a thing between Vince and me lately. It had all started when I was complaining to Vince that I didn't get how Joe Blanton could always dominate the Cubs, because he was so terrible. Then Vince made me Google Joe's stats to show me that he wasn't nearly as bad as I'd thought.

But that was the thing: numbers weren't everything in baseball, because if they were, then Barry Bonds and Pete Rose would have been no-brainer, first-ballot Hall of Famers, and a guy like Derek Jeter would simply be a really good shortstop and not a modern-day legend. Baseball was more than just numbers; it was also about intangibles and respect. It was about playing the game the right way, which was to play smart and play for the team and not to pad your own personal numbers. To play with grit and get the job done, which meant taking one on the chin and losing a couple teeth if that's what it takes to get a guy to second base. Or at least that's what I thought. Vince was much more of a numbers guy. To him the numbers didn't lie. That's what he always told me anyway. "Mac, the numbers don't lie." He thought he could win any argument with that line.

Anyways, all of that is beside the point. What mattered was that having a pitcher like Joe Blanton at the plate with the bases loaded was about as miserable a situation as you could put yourself in as a baseball team. He was like 95 percent likely to strike out three times in a single at bat, which of course isn't possible, but with Joe any dubious feat was possible. And that's kind of what we were dealing with here with Dr. George now showing up. It felt like he was on our team but would undoubtedly cost us the game.

Vince and I met up at my locker after school to head over to the gym for baseball tryouts. For the next few weeks it was going to be only for pitchers and catchers, kind of like how they always report first for Spring Training in the majors. The position player tryouts weren't for another month or so, when the temperature outside would warm up a little.

We were both especially curious to see how this would go, considering how we'd now heard two completely different versions of what the new coach was supposedly like. Mr. Kjelson generally had a good reputation, but after what Trixie Von Parkway told us earlier, I wasn't too sure what to expect.

I did not expect him to look so small, that's for sure. That's the first thing I noticed when we stepped inside the gym. He was just barely taller than some of the seventh and eighth graders around him. There was a pile of catcher gear in the middle of the floor and a bag of baseballs at his feet.

"Come on in here, guys." Mr. Kjelson waved us over. We walked over and joined the group of kids standing around him.

Other than being fairly short and small, Mr. Kjelson was a pretty normal-looking guy. He seemed to be a little younger than my dad and had short hair that looked like it hadn't been combed in a while. He was wearing jeans and a T-shirt, and he did not have a whistle like most coaches do, which I was pretty happy to see. Seriously, most coaches abused their whistles worse than the Cubs general manager abused his payroll, which could get annoying really quickly.

I scanned the other kids in attendance. It was pretty tough to make the team as a sixth grader. In fact, there was only one other sixth grader there, a kid named Tazaharu Matsuko, a foreign exchange student from Japan. Everybody at our school just called him Taz.

"Okay, everybody, this is the first day of tryouts for pitchers and catchers. Today I just kind of want you all to take it easy. Don't worry about blowing me away with your ninety-mile-per-hour gun. Just focus on hitting your spots and getting loose. No pressure today, right? Now, let's have the pitchers all group over here and the catchers here."

There were about seven of us catchers and more than

twenty pitchers. He said we'd be rotating. Kjelson lined us catchers up along the gym on one end where he had laid down some rubber mats, then took the pitchers the correct distance to the other end. He had placed a piece of red tape earlier that he must have measured as the fifty-four feet between the plate and mound.

He explained how the rotation system would work. Five pitches per catcher then switch. Just light throwing for the first twenty or thirty minutes. Try to hit the glove, nothing more, nothing less.

"And remember, we're all trying to make the same team, so I don't want to see any Barrett and Zambrano action, okay?"

A few of us chuckled. I raised my hand. "You're a Cubs fan, Coach?"

He smirked at me, the kind of empty and sad smile that only another Cubs fan could recognize. "Unfortunately I am."

I shook my head in sympathy, but really I was pretty happy. Being a Cubs fan was like a sacred bond. It was like a lifelong connection to every other Cubs fan that was almost stronger than being actual family because real families usually don't suffer as much together as Cubs fans do. Being stuck in crappy situations seems to bring people together for some reason, so being Cubs fans brought us all together each and every year. It was good to have that connection with our potential coach.

And I had to admit it . . . there was no way a Cubs fan could be as awful a guy as Trixie had said Kjelson was.

Tryouts went well, I thought. Some kids were clearly rusty, and so we catchers spent a lot of time blocking balls and retrieving the ones we missed, which bounced all over the hard gym floor. It was pretty painful and difficult trying to block bad pitches in that gym, but none of us complained.

The pitchers did some light throwing and then moved on to fastballs. No breaking stuff for the first try-out. Vince was clearly the best kid I caught. He hit my glove every time; I swear I never had to move even an inch. Also, he threw harder than most of the other kids, and he didn't even come close to throwing as hard as I knew he could. I think Kjelson was impressed, too, because he seemed to spend extra time watching Vince pitch, and he gave more pointers to him than to the other kids, which was a good sign.

Kjelson called over Vince, Taz, and me after he dismissed everyone else.

"I was really impressed with what I saw today out of you three," he said. "It's going to be tough for three sixth graders to make the team, I can't lie about that, but if you all keep it up, there's definitely a chance it could happen this year."

"Thanks, Coach," I said, and Taz gave a short nod.

Then Kjelson smiled and said, "I mean, if Joe Blanton can actually make a major league rotation, let alone one that includes Oswalt, Lee, Hamels, and Halladay, then anything is possible, right?"

Vince and I laughed, and Taz just kind of nodded again. No doubt now that Kjelson was going to be a great coach if we were lucky enough to make the team. I mean, Joe Blanton wasn't exactly a household name. I couldn't believe he'd just dissed him like Vince or I would have done in that same spot. I glanced at Vince, and I could tell he was thinking the same thing, even though he was always defending Joe Blanton because Vince was such a sucker for numbers.

"Hey, not that I'm arguing about us being able to make the team," Vince said, "but Joe Blanton once struck out eleven batters in a single inning, so I'd watch what you say."

This, of course, was not even close to being true, but that was just how Vince's humor worked. I only hoped Mr. Kjelson would realize that or Vince was going to look like a mouthy jerk. But once again I probably hadn't given Mr. K. enough credit because he laughed so hard, you'd have thought that Vince had just made the single best joke in baseball history.

* * *

Later that night Vince, Joe, and I met up with Tyrell Alishouse outside the school. Tyrell was my ace in the hole. He was the best thing a guy like me could have on his payroll. He specialized in all types of surveillance.

I had a key to get us into the school through the East Wing entrance, due to a sweet deal I'd made with the janitor several years ago. We were there now to set up video cameras, something I'd intended to do a long time ago but had never really had the funds for. Since we still had all our Cubs game funds from last season and had the sudden burst of customers lately *and* Dr. George had just shown up out of nowhere, now was the best time to do it.

Tyrell had access to all kinds of awesome spy stuff that he sold to us for a pretty good price, plus a small fee for installation. We bought two small cameras from him. They were wireless and transmitted to digital recorders that we could hide inside the empty toilet tank in our office, in the first stall from the high window.

We set up the first camera in the corner so that it captured pretty much the entire bathroom but, most important, the fourth stall and trash can where we kept our Books and the Tom Petty cash, which was a lock-box containing a few hundred dollars that we used for day-to-day business. The rest of the cash was stored in my bedroom closet behind a false panel in the wall.

Vince and I boosted Tyrell to the ceiling, each of us holding one foot. He was able to conceal the first camera pretty well amid all of the cobwebs and dust and who knows what else that had collected up there over the years.

The second camera was installed just outside the bathroom so we would have a recording of every person who ever came in or out of our office. Tyrell was able to position that one on top of the red fire alarm so that you could see it only if you knew to look for it; otherwise it looked just like a part of the fire alarm.

"And these will have sound?" I asked as we tested out the transmission to the digital recorders by hooking up one of the DVRs to a small handheld TV that Tyrell had brought.

Tyrell grinned and turned on the TV. Then suddenly there we were on the screen, the three of us standing just outside my office. Tyrell hit Play, and the last few minutes played out on the screen. The camera had recorded everything we said.

"They come with ultra-sonic digital microphones capable of recording conversations from up to a hundred feet away," he said. "Also, they have motion sensors, so they only record if they detect movement. That way you don't just burn through all of the space on the DVRs every night. The DVRs will need to be brought home every few weeks to be backed up and emptied."

"Wow. Thanks, Tyrell," Vince said. I nodded.

I took off my backpack and got out the funds I'd brought from home to pay Tyrell. Even thought he was giving us a good price, this stuff was still setting us back a pretty good chunk of money. But it was worth it for better peace of mind. That's what my dad had told my mom when he convinced her to get a security system installed a few months ago after our house had been vandalized.

Of course it was my fault that it had gotten vandalized, but I wasn't going to fess up to that to save my dad a few hundred bucks or whatever it was that his system cost. Once my dad was set on getting some new gadget, there was no stopping him anyway. He probably spent like ten grand a month on new phones because he was obsessed with always having the best one. I mean, who cares if your phone is waterproof up to ten feet or fireproof for up to ten minutes? It's not like you'll be making phone calls from the middle of a raging inferno or from the bottom of a lake.

I shook my head while fiddling with Tyrell's cool miniature TV. Some people and their weird technology obsession. Seriously . . .

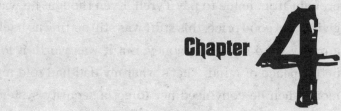

Chapter 4

Wednesday—The Fourth Stall

We were swamped with new customers right away at early recess the next morning. The first was this tall lanky kid. He was almost as tall as Joe but probably weighed half as much. I almost wanted to, like, string up a flag on him, he was so tall and skinny.

"Have a seat." I motioned to the ridiculously small chair across from me. He looked at it like a big-game hunter might look at a water gun. Then he sighed and lowered himself into the chair. I had to stifle a laugh when his knees almost hit his chin. I felt bad for not having better accommodations, but I wasn't used to living skyscrapers walking into my office.

"Sorry about the chair," I said after he told me his name was Timmy B.

He shrugged.

"So what's on your mind?"

"It's our coach," he said. I assumed he meant basketball coach since football season was over and the only two sports going on right now were basketball and swimming. He could have been a swimmer, sure, but something told me this kid was a basketball player. Call it a hunch.

I motioned for him to continue.

"Well, he's kind of been running up the score on people lately. And, I mean, of course it feels good to win and everything, but I feel bad for the bench guys. Me and the other four starters have been playing almost the whole time, even when we're up by like forty points."

I nodded. I'd even noticed that myself. Vince and I tried to catch as many of the home basketball games as we could. Everybody did. Our basketball team was one of the best in the region, maybe in the whole state. In fact, I thought our team could even beat some of the high school teams in the area.

I guess it was pretty easy to run up the score when you're that good. I know the crowd mostly loved it. But the thing is, even I had noticed how much the coach was rubbing it in. I mean, when you're up 68 to 15, like we were the Friday night before last, then you know your starters shouldn't be in the game anymore. That's part of why I loved baseball so much more than basketball: baseball players have some class. I mean, you'd never see a baseball team stealing bases and dropping sac bunts in the seventh inning while up by ten runs.

"So . . ." I said, not sure exactly what he wanted. I agreed with him, sure, but I didn't see why it was so bad for him that he got to play all game and pad his stats.

"Well, I just feel bad, you know? Like one of our backup forwards, Leonard Leery, well, he worked pretty hard to make the team this year despite the fact that he's not very athletic—and he still hasn't even gotten into a game once. I feel bad for the kid."

"Wait, wait, Leonard Leery made the team?" I asked.

Timmy B. nodded.

Leonard Leery was a nice guy, but he was about as uncoordinated as an ostrich with no legs, which means about what it sounds like: he was equivalent to a bird body with a long neck and tiny head flopping around on the ground—just imagine trying to throw a chest pass to that. Oh, and he's also about four feet tall, which if you know anything about basketball makes him about as good a forward as a jug of Kool-Aid.

I think Timmy B. could see that I was struggling with the concept of wanting to get Leonard Leery more playing time, especially when our team had a reputation for being so stellar.

"Look, I know Leonard stinks," he said, "but that's beside the point. He worked really hard to make the team, and I kinda respect that he was willing to even try, you know? A lot of nerds like Leonard just sit around and wish they could play sports and make fun of us for being dumb just because they have no athletic ability, but he just went for it. It's not like he's so bad that he'll lose us the game in just a couple minutes of playing time when we're already up by over forty points. Right? He hasn't gotten to play a single second, Mac, and that's just not right. Hardly any of the bench guys have played."

He definitely had a point.

"Do you think you can get some of the bench guys some playing time? I mean, just because I heard Leonard call our team a 'squadron,' the basketball the 'spheroid game-piece,' the hoop the 'goal-scoring receptacle,' and a jump shot a 'levitating toss throw' doesn't mean he shouldn't get to play."

Then we both burst out laughing. Leonard was just so nerdy, it was kind of hard not to like the kid for some reason.

"I'll do what I can, Timmy B.," I said. "I'll even do this one pro bono, since it's more like a charity case than you asking for something for yourself."

"Uh, thanks, I think. . . ."

"Pro bono means for free," I said, noting his furrowed brow.

"Oh, cool. Thanks a bunch, Mac."

I nodded, but I knew this would be tough. Now I had both a job to get a teacher off someone's back and one to change a coach's policy on end-of-game tactics. These were major league problems, so to have more than one made them even more challenging. But if anybody could pull it off, it would be Vince and I.

Timmy B. nodded good-bye and then slowly lifted himself up from the tiny chair and left my office.

The rest of recess didn't get much better as far as getting any easy problems. A few more kids complained about finding poop in their lockers, though luckily they weren't quite as desperate and manic as Tony had been about it.

We also had a real meathead-jock type kid come in and complain about having to do "sissy stuff" in gym class lately. Like dancing and Hula-Hoop and limbo and parachuting and stuff like that. I actually thought the last one sounded pretty cool until I found out that it involved the class grabbing a parachute and throwing it in the air until it inflated. That still sounded kind of cool, but this kid was the sort of kid who wasn't happy unless gym class somehow involved him pelting nerdy kids in the face with rubber balls thrown at teeth-shattering speeds, which he somehow managed to do while playing just about any sport and not just dodgeball.

Another issue that several kids had come to me for that day was the upcoming SMARTs that Dr. George had talked about the day before. Kids had been hearing rumors that the tests were really tough. Our school was scheduled to take them all next week. Apparently they were a pretty big deal because a lot of kids were coming to me wondering if I could get them test answers. I wasn't sure if I'd be able to swing that since the tests were administered by someone outside of the school system. I told them I'd look into it, but I wasn't as worried as they were. Like I said before, kids like to overreact when it comes to tests. Our school was pretty smart; I was sure we'd do well.

More than just making me extra busy (and, hopefully, extra wealthy), all of this business had me wondering what was up. The weird school lunches, poop in kids' lockers, a sadistic basketball coach, a science teacher who may or may not be terrorizing someone, a new vice principal who happened to be a Lord of Punishment . . . Could all of these things really just be coincidence? I wasn't sure how they could be related, except that it seemed likely that Dr. George had been brought in to fix up some of these things. Some of these problems were likely the other issues that Dickerson had referenced during the assembly. But I had a feeling something was up. One way or the other I intended to find out.

Chapter 5

Wednesday—The Cafeteria

At lunch that day we had to close up the office so we could start working on some of the recent cases coming in. Vince and I started out by dealing with Jonah's problem and actually going to the cafeteria for lunch. Well, okay, we weren't ever going to eat the school lunch, but we at least got in line like everybody else.

"Hey, check it out," Vince said, pointing at the dry-erase board on the wall.

The sign read:

TODAY'S LUNCH
Monte Cristo with Raspberry Preserves
and Powdered Sugar

Double-Battered Onion Rings with
Creamy Dipping Sauce
Double-Chocolate Fudge Milk Shake

"That sounds pretty good. Except, what the heck is a Monte Crispo?" I said.

"It's Monte *Cris-To*," Vince said. "It's basically a huge triple-decker turkey and cheese sandwich that's battered and deep-fried with jam and powdered sugar on top."

After I picked up my lower jaw off the floor, I said, "No wonder Jonah was freaking out so hard. I wonder how many calories are in one of those things?"

Vince shrugged. "Probably like five thousand or something; I don't know."

A few girls behind us overheard me and started giggling. Then I noticed that one of them was Trixie, and I felt my face turn red so quickly, it was like someone had doused it with gasoline and then lit a match on my teeth.

"Watching your figure, Mac?" Trixie asked. Her friends giggled madly at this.

I shook my head. Normally I'd just let the joke and the giggling go, but I didn't want Trixie to think I was anything like Jonah. "I'm on a case, actually."

But this only made them laugh harder. Even Vince

smirked, and he slapped my shoulder as we turned away from Trixie and her friends. I heard one of them say the word "adorable," which was then followed by more laughter. I didn't really appreciate being likened to a stuffed animal or puppy or something, but I figured it was best just to keep my mouth shut at that point.

"So why are they serving this stuff? Everybody knows that school lunches are supposed to be disgusting," I whispered.

"I don't know. Do you really think we can get them to stop? Even if we do, kids are going to hate us, Mac," Vince said.

I looked across the lunchroom. It was true. Kids were stuffing their faces with thick, golden onion rings, their hands slick and yellow with oil. Grease ran from their mouths and dripped off chins onto shirts as bites were taken from giant battered sandwiches. Some kids with crinkled noses used their forks to pick at the jam sitting atop their Monte Cristos, but their disgust at the greasy sandwich didn't stop them from practically dunking their whole heads into bucket-sized milk shakes.

Vince was right. If we actually got the lunches to return to normal and word ever got out that we were to blame, we'd be as good as dead.

"Well, we should still probably at least see what's going on, right?" I said.

Vince nodded.

We each grabbed a lunch tray and moved through the line.

The first lunch lady was actually not a lunch lady at all. It was a small old man with the biggest pair of glasses I'd ever seen. The frames were red and almost as thick as a school textbook, and the lenses themselves were the size of hockey pucks.

He slapped a huge pile of onion rings onto my tray with a pair of glowing, greasy tongs.

"Excuse me," I said. "Not that I'm complaining, but why are you serving us such good food lately?"

He looked at me, his eyes magnified by the lenses so that they filled his entire face. Then without a word he plopped another small army of onion rings atop the ones already on my tray.

"No, no, I don't want more. I was just wondering . . ."

He snatched up more onion rings with the tongs, so I decided to move on before I had an entire mountain range of thick golden hoops on my tray.

I looked at Vince, who was grinning.

The next lunch lady gave us our sandwiches, which had to weigh close to five pounds each, considering the noise they made when they hit our trays. Then at the end there was a large tray with milk shakes on it. We each took one. We handed the last lunch lady our school

IDs and she scanned them into the computer.

"Can I ask you something?" I said after she handed back my ID.

She tilted her head toward me as if she was too tired to actually turn and face me.

"I was looking forward to a healthy and nutritious meal like always, and I was wondering why you're serving this instead?"

Her face didn't move. Not even a smile or a blink. Then she said, "Look, kid, you get what you get, okay?"

"But who sets the menu?" Vince asked.

The lunch lady shrugged.

"How can you not know? How do you know what to make? Who tells you? Where does this food come from?"

"Hey, I don't need this, okay? Next, please," she called out, looking past me now.

I sighed and looked at Vince. He tilted his head toward the swinging doors behind the ticket lady.

I nodded, and we moved on. After a few more feet we veered back around and slipped through the doors into the kitchen.

In the back sat four gigantic vats of steaming grease. They were each the size of a bathtub but twice as deep. A man with a pretty big stomach and two red-haired old ladies were dipping huge baskets of sandwiches and frozen onion rings into the bathtubs of oil.

One of the red-haired ladies turned.

"Hey, you can't be back here," she said.

"Hi!" I said as friendly as I could. "We're doing a report on school nutrition for our class newspaper. How does this lunch fit in with the state regulations?"

"What?" the other redheaded lady asked.

"You can't be back here," the first one said again.

"What are your names?" the man with the large belly said.

I set my tray on the counter because my arms were getting tired from holding what was surely thirty pounds of food.

"Who makes the menu choices here?" Vince asked.

"What?" Redhead Number Two said again.

"You can't be back here," repeated the first one.

"What are your names?" the man said again, putting down his fry basket.

I was beginning to wonder if the school had somehow invented robot cooks. But then that theory went out the window when Redhead Number Two put down her own basket and moved toward us. This time she finally said something other than "What?"

"Get out of here, right now!"

"But our report—" I started.

"I don't care. Get out. Now!" she yelled.

As we shuffled back out into the cafeteria, I heard Redhead Number One say, "They weren't supposed to be back here."

"Well, that was pretty unproductive," Vince said.

"Oh, like you helped any. The one time a quote from your grandma might have actually helped us and you just stood there."

"Well, you know what she'd say now, don't you?"

I couldn't help but laugh. "No, but I bet I'm going to find out, right?"

"She'd say, 'When the sun rises to the north and sets to the turkey, then you'd better get ready for a whole lot of bananas wearing cowboy hats.'"

I shook my head and fought back another laugh.

"Well, one thing's for sure: I'm not touching that lunchroom business again," I said. "I'm thinking we just find a way to get Jonah his healthy food each day and let everybody else enjoy the fried stuff while it lasts."

"Good thinking. Then we need to start working on the Kjelson case. It won't be long before Trixie comes back to complain about him again. The way she described him makes Joseph Goebbels seem like Mister Rogers, but from what we've heard and witnessed during practice, he's a pretty cool guy. And a Cubs fan."

"Who and Mister Rogers?" I asked.

"He's— Ah, never mind. Don't you read or pay attention in class ever?" Vince said.

"Hey, I've got better things to do. Like run my business to pay for all your video games and books and stuff."

"Touché," Vince said with a grin.

I wasn't sure what "tooshay" meant exactly. But whatever he was saying, he was right: the Kjelson problem was probably the most perplexing at this point. We'd have to look into that later that day if we could. The thing was, I just wasn't sure when we'd find time since our whole day was pretty much booked solid already.

From the cafeteria we headed to Tony Adrian's locker to investigate. The Hutt was there just finishing up his cleaning duties while Tony stood behind him several feet away, practically dancing he looked so anxious.

"Almost done," the Hutt slurred. Not only did this kid look like Jabba the Hutt, but he also sounded just like him, too.

In one hand he held a pile of little black pellets; with the other he was picking more up from the bottom of the locker. I made a mental note never to shake that kid's hand again. I had to say, I knew the Hutt was nasty, but I couldn't believe he hadn't used gloves or even a plastic bag. I think Tony Adrian was thinking the same thing because he was practically convulsing behind him. I thought for sure Tony was going to break into a seizure at any moment.

I looked at the rest of his locker. It was like a hospital or something. Every item inside was carefully wrapped in plastic. And there were stacks of small plastic Tupperware containers with various items inside, such as pencils and erasers and pens. Everything was neatly stacked and symmetrical like a tessellation or pattern or something. I couldn't decide right then who was actually the weirder kid: the Hutt or Tony.

"All done," the Hutt sloshed. He carried his pile of poop to a nearby trash can. When he got back, he held out his hand for me to shake. "Thanks for the job."

I hesitated. On one hand it was unprofessional not to shake hands after a business transaction, but on the other that hand had just seconds ago been holding a pile of poop the size of a softball. But in the end my business sense won out. I couldn't help it: I like to run a sound operation.

I shook the Hutt's hand, which was warm and kind of sticky, and I almost gagged. Then the Hutt grinned at me and said, "Let me know when it needs to be cleaned again." He turned and walked down the hall, slapping kids on the back as he went. Then at the end of the hallway I could have sworn I saw him stick his hand into his mouth for some inexplicable reason.

"Mac, what did you just do?" Vince said through laughter. "Remind me to never ever share food with you again. Also, I don't think you can be my catcher anymore. I mean, sure, spitballs have some extra action to them, but I'm not so sure that poop-balls give us any competitive advantage besides maybe kids whiffing on purpose so they don't get fecal matter on their bats."

"Towel," I said. Then I said it again perhaps more loudly than necessary, "Towel. Towel!"

I motioned desperately for Tony to get me one of his little wipes while holding my hand out in front me as if I had the Cheese Touch from this hilarious Wimpy Kid book that I read once. I grabbed my forearm with my other hand like a tourniquet to keep the poop from spreading to the rest of my body. Tony handed a towelette to me and then took several steps back. I wiped my hand with the wet towel, scrubbing every finger and my palm as if I was trying to rub all of my skin right off, which was almost the case. Then I asked for another towel and repeated the process until I was sure my hand was as clean as it would ever get.

Meanwhile Tony was on the floor near his locker scrubbing the bottom with a bottle of cleaner that he'd had inside. He worked furiously but in a controlled and efficient manner, as if this was something he did everyday anyway, with or without poop.

When he was done, he said, "Thanks, Mac. I hope you figure out soon how this is happening."

"We will," I said.

Vince and I examined the locker thoroughly with a flashlight that Vince had brought with him. We didn't see any possible entrance or exit for small animals. It was baffling. How was the poop getting in there?

"What do you think?" I asked him.

"Well," Vince said, "let's lay down some humane, kill-free traps. Probably best to find out what kind of animal it is first."

I nodded. As usual Vince had a great idea. "All right, we'll have Joe come by tomorrow right before the first bell to lay some down. Can you meet him here?"

Tony nodded. "Sounds good," he said, wiping his hands with another towel.

Chapter 6

Wednesday—Mr. Skari's Classroom

Later that day in class Mr. Skari announced that for the next few days we'd be reviewing materials specifically for SMART preparation. He said it was very important that we do well. And if he was willing to change his class schedule around to help us prepare, then it really must be an important test—because Mr. Skari hated to deviate from his class schedule. One time he even came to school with a shattered arm. Apparently he'd slipped on the ice in his driveway that morning and broken it. Mr. Skari is like six and a half feet tall, so when a guy like that falls, it usually ends in broken limbs. But he was so obsessed with staying on schedule that he didn't even go to the hospital until after school that day. Some kids claim they could even see bone sticking out of his arm through the makeshift sling he'd made, but there was no way that was true. Right?

Anyways, the point is if Mr. Skari was willing to deviate from his regular class schedule for this test, then that meant it really was a *big* deal.

After talking about some math subjects that would be on the test, he handed out this huge packet of worksheets to complete for the rest of the day. Everybody groaned, even me. Packets are the worst. Nobody likes packets. Well, except for Garret Henley—he loves packets, but he also loves all homework, eating string cheese dipped in grape jelly, and watching the Public Access TV channel. So his opinion doesn't count for much.

"Christian?" Mr. Skari said a few minutes after handing out our packets.

I looked up from my math assignment with a frown. It was never a good sign to have the teacher say your name during classwork time. Mr. Skari motioned for me to come to his desk.

As I got up, he said, "Better grab your stuff."

That was an even worse sign.

I collected my things, threw them into my backpack, and approached his desk.

"Yeah?"

"You need to go see Dr. George."

"Why?"

Mr. Skari gave me one of those looks that said, *You know why.* For the most part Mr. Skari and I got along pretty well. For him being a teacher anyways. So he'd probably tell me if he knew exactly why I needed to go see Dr. George.

He handed me my hall pass and I headed off toward the administration offices.

The place where happiness goes to die.

So it seemed I was going to get my first meeting with the new vice principal. I would get to see what he was all about firsthand. I'm going to admit that I was a little nervous. I mean, you don't get reputations like Dr. George's by being an empty threat.

As bad as Head Principal Dickerson was, Dr. George would probably be even worse. They were both clearly old cranky guys with little to no hair whose faces would shatter into gory messes of blood and skin if they ever smiled, but the difference was that Dickerson was kind of a bumbling idiot, whereas Dr. George had a reputation for being razor sharp, the sort of guy you couldn't just talk your way around. He was still a doctor, after all, even if it was the fake kind.

I shuffled inside the door to the administration offices, and the secretary held out her hand. I wasn't sure if she wanted me to shake it or something, but then I looked at the hall pass clutched in my own hand and held it out to her. She snatched it away as if she thought I might pull it back at any moment.

I had never been called to the principal's office before. I was just a simple businessman, not a troublemaker.

The secretary pointed at a door to my left.

The silence could have suffocated me.

The door was huge, but the nameplate on it was tiny and slightly crooked. I reached to knock, but the door opened before I could. He'd been expecting me, I guessed.

Dr. George held the door open and swept his other hand toward a chair across from his desk. I sat down. He closed the office door and sat across from me. He was a normal-sized guy. He had a lot of wrinkles, and his eyes moved too much, but other than that and his two-toned fake hair, he looked just like any other crusty old guy.

We sat there looking at each other for a while. His breathing was loud and his nose wheezed with each exhale. He stared right at me, and I tried to hold his gaze as long as I could, but it was hard. The guy was making me nervous—even more so than adults usually do. What was his game?

"Well?" he said finally.

"Well," I said back.

He frowned.

"What do you have to say for yourself?" he said.

"For what?" I dug my fingers into the wooden arm-rests on my chair.

"Don't play games with me, Mr. Barrett."

"I'm not playing games. I wish I were," I said.

He pounded a fist on the desk. "I'm tired of this attitude from you kids! Show some respect!"

He startled me, and I jumped, suddenly more afraid than I ever expected to be in my own school. His voice echoed deep into my brain even after he'd finished yelling.

"I'm sorry, sir, I just don't know what I did wrong."

"You don't."

"No."

He sighed and leaned back in his chair. He grabbed a folder from a drawer behind him and slapped it onto the desk. Then he leafed through it briefly before closing it again. He was making a big show and I knew it.

"You were caught trespassing in the kitchen," he said, pounding the folder with his index finger to emphasize each word. "We're not going to tolerate any funny business around here anymore. None."

"Oh, that. Yeah. I wasn't trespassing, I was doing research for—"

"That'll be all," he said, and turned his chair so that he was facing his computer.

I got up and somehow ended up back in class, though I don't remember actually walking there. Other than it causing me to miss baseball tryouts, I didn't really care at all about the detention; I'd just use that time to work on some of my current cases. But I was concerned about the fact that the Administration was now on my tail. It'd been hard enough to keep up with business anyways; now I had to worry about being cased by Suits. All I could do, though, was be more careful and hope that Dr. George really didn't have a clue what was going on, that it had just been an empty threat.

Vince got detention, too, for the cafeteria stunt. But he hadn't gotten any cryptic threats from Dr. George, just the standard lecture and detention. He didn't like what I told him at the start of afternoon recess that day.

"What are we going to do? We've never had the Administration on our tails before," Vince said. "This is, like, almost worse than that one time I tried to prove that gravity was a myth using nothing but a box of toothpicks, the big oak tree in my backyard, four packages of grape Kool-Aid, and a lawn gnome with a missing hand."

"I remember that," Joe said.

I did, too, and it had been pretty funny, aside from

Vince's crooked ankle and two months of him in a cast ordering me around and whining about being one limb down. But I really wasn't in a laughing mood just then.

"I guess the only thing we can do is keep focusing on our current customers. And also be more careful," I said. "Hey, Fred?"

"Yeah?"

"How about for a while you can be our official look-out instead of keeping records? You can sit in the first stall and watch the hall camera through a small portable TV hooked up to the DVR. You can watch the end of the west hall and tell us if a Suit or teacher is coming. Then maybe we can get Brady to watch the west entrance near my office."

"Sure, Mac," Fred said.

"That sounds like a plan," Vince said.

"Then maybe today after detention, Vince and I will take a look around Mr. Kjelson's office. See what we can find."

"What about baseball tryouts today, Mac?" Vince asked. "We're going to miss due to detention. The last thing we need as sixth graders trying to make the team is to give the coach any reason at all to cut us."

I thought about that. "We'll just have to talk to Kjelson and make up for it on the field . . . or in the gym or—you know what I mean."

Vince nodded but still looked concerned.

"All right. There's a line forming outside, so let's open up for business for the rest of recess," I said.

Our first customer that day was a dual customer— and an odd pair to be showing up together, at that. A lanky, pale kid and a small kid with neat hair, a collared shirt, and a sweater vest with a goose on it stepped into my office. They were Great White and Kitten, two of the more notorious bullies in the school.

Great White was British and had blond hair and pale skin. He also had a real mean streak and was one of the best fighters and toughest kids in the school. Kitten was meek and mild with a soft voice and neat clothes. But his appearance was deceiving. He was quite possibly the most insane person in the entire state. He probably belonged in a psych ward. Seriously, if he and I didn't get along so well and he hadn't helped my business so much in the past, I'd have turned him in to state officials a long time ago. If you crossed him, he was more dangerous than anyone in the city, probably. He'd eat your dog right in front of you with a knife and fork and a napkin tucked under his collar if you made him mad enough. But he and Great White weren't friends, so it was weird to see them together like this.

"Have a seat," I told them.

They sat down in the two chairs across from me. For

the first time I noticed that Great White had a black eye and a large bandage on his neck. I remembered that some kids had complained about him picking a lot of fights lately due to the lack of punishment from the school. I wondered if this could be related.

"What seems to be the problem?" I asked.

"Well, besides the fact that this little git over here bit me in me neck like some sort of vampire?" Great White said.

"You bit him in the neck?" I said to Kitten.

Kitten looked calm, collected, and small as usual. "He started the fight. I just finished it," he said quietly.

I held back a laugh. Didn't Great White know any better than to mess with Kitten? "So why are you both here? Also, if you started the fight, Great White . . ."

"No, no, I'm not, like, here to tattle on the little psycho. We're here because of the punishment we got for scrapping on school property, yeah? I mean, we was just knockin' about, minding our own business, and then some little squealer had to go and tattle on us. Anyway, lately I is only be gettin' like two days' detention, tops, for fighting, but now this Dr. George guy be giving us two weeks' detention for one little scrap!"

I looked at Kitten for confirmation and he nodded. "Yeah, I've never gotten two full weeks for simply defending myself."

So George was apparently pretty serious about ending the funny business in our school. Which was fine, in a way, but he was a direct threat to my business and maybe even more than that.

It was official. I had to get rid of Dr. George.

"I'll see what I can do," I said. I suddenly felt kind of like I was suffocating. I just didn't have the manpower to handle all of these problems. Getting teachers and coaches fired was hard enough, but now I had to worry about getting rid of a Suit? I'd never messed with the Administration before, and I didn't exactly want to start, but it was looking like I might not have a choice.

Chapter 7

Wednesday—The Detention Room

"Okay, Vince, are you ready?" I asked.

"When aren't I? Seriously, Mac. We always ask each other if we're ready and we always are."

"Good point."

"Quiet down! This is detention not social hour," Mr. Daniels said from behind his computer.

Mr. Daniels had been the detention warden for as long as anyone could remember. He always just sat behind his computer playing games or maybe doing stuff we didn't even want to know about, rarely even looking up at the kids sitting in detention. And he would generally yell at us every fifteen minutes to quiet down but never actually handed out any more punishment. That bit about "social hour" was his signature line. He'd yell that exact same line to a room filled with nothing but silence and a few sleeping eighth graders. Everybody had figured out long ago that Mr. Daniels didn't really pay any attention to us at all.

"Anyways," I continued in a voice just above a whisper, "who was the last Cub to hit for the cycle?"

Vince scoffed. "Are you insulting me?"

"Whatever, it's not that easy."

Vince gave me a look that said, *Yes it is.*

"Even my grandma could get this one, and she thinks that baseball is some sort of satanic ritual invented in 1812 by Communist kangaroos to help an alien tribe of sea creatures called Trout Mask Replicas build the ancient pyramids."

I tried desperately to hold in my laughter.

"It was Mark Grace, beloved first-baseman-turned-Diamondback traitor," he said.

I nodded reluctantly.

"You'll never—" Something at the door caught Vince's eye.

I spun around in my desk, and there she was: Trixie Von Parkway. Otherwise known as the dark-haired girl who'd come to see me in my office yesterday and who'd made fun of me with her friends in the cafeteria today. Obviously Trixie wasn't her real name, but

I hadn't gotten around to having Tyrell find out what it really was just yet.

She slithered into the room, looking as poisonous as ever, and handed Mr. Daniels her detention slip.

He glanced at it and grunted. "Have a seat and work on homework quietly. This is detention not social hour."

The dark-haired girl moved past me without any kind of acknowledgment and sat right behind us. We turned around and stared at her as she dug through her backpack and removed a notebook. Then her eyes met ours.

"Hey, you two freaks got a problem?" she said.

"Sorry," I mumbled, and turned around.

Vince followed suit. We glanced at each other and shrugged.

"Oh, wait. It's just you," she said. "I didn't recognize you."

I turned around again. "What do you mean, 'just me'?"

"I thought you were just two guys with ridiculous crushes on me or something, that's all."

My face grew hot.

"So about my problem. Have you two done *anything* yet besides whine about calories all day? Oh, wait, *obviously* not, being that I'm in detention right now," she said.

"Kjelson put you here?"

"What do you think? Do you think I'm normally in detention? That I'm a bad girl? Is that what you think?" She seemed to be getting dangerously close to tears and anger all at once. She was possibly the scariest person I'd ever met—about as calm and predictable as a city-leveling tornado.

"No, no. I just thought . . ." I started to apologize.

Then she started laughing. "You should see your face. I'm just kidding around with you, Mac."

I tried to laugh with her. Vince had no problems laughing at me either. I glared at him and he just laughed even harder.

"Quiet down! This is detention not social hour," Mr. Daniels yelled.

"Wow, he just gave the three forty-five warning at three forty-four," Vince said. "He's ahead of schedule."

Trixie giggled madly at this.

For the first time ever I wanted Vince to stop talking, but I honestly couldn't tell you why; it had been a pretty funny thing to say.

"Seriously, though, when are you going to get Kjelson off my back? This is my fourth day of detention in a row because of him. I didn't even do anything wrong at all today. He just gave me detention."

"You had to have done something," I said. "Teachers can't just give out detention for no reason."

She scoffed at me like I was an idiot. "Oh no? Then why am I here? I swear, I was just sitting in class taking notes. I think maybe my pencil broke or something and made a noise because suddenly he was like, 'Trixie, no talking!' And I was shocked, so I didn't really say anything. I just kind of sighed. Then he was like, 'That's it! Detention again, young lady!' So I was like, 'But I didn't do anything!' You know? Because I hadn't. But he got all red in the face and was sputtering like a dying motorcycle and said, 'Okay, that's two days of detention!' So I started to protest, but he was just on a roll, you know? He started screaming, 'I'm tired of your attitude! Another outburst and you are out of here for good!' So what was I to do? I need to pass that class to graduate and go on to high school. So I shut up and took my detention."

That sounded pretty horrible, but it also didn't sound like Kjelson at all.

"That kind of reminds me of this one time that my grandma wouldn't stop cursing in church," Vince said. I groaned. He had a Grandma story for *everything*. "We were like, 'Grandma, you have to be quiet. We'll get kicked out.' But she just went on ranting and raving, with every other word being a swearword, about how her Lucky Charms had been mocking her during breakfast. But the best part is that she didn't even have Lucky

Charms that morning. She had, like, waffles with hand lotion on them or something. Anyways, she didn't stop, so we got kicked out." He laughed. "How many people do you know who got kicked out of church?"

Instead of getting annoyed at how pointless his story was like I thought she would, Trixie actually laughed. She and Vince were cracking up together.

"Quiet down," Mr. Daniels barked. "This is detention not social hour!"

That was just like Vince, too. Always telling lame stories when there were more pressing issues. Sometimes I wished he could just not tell a Grandma story for once. But I still had to admit that most of the time I found them pretty funny. Even this one was pretty funny.

"Well, anyways, we're working on it for you," I said over their laughter. "It takes time to get to teachers; it's only been two days. Rome wasn't burned down in a day, you know."

"Gosh, you are a cutie," she said.

I blushed. "What . . ."

Vince nudged me. "It goes, 'Rome wasn't *built* in a day,' Mac."

I blushed even more, and I turned around to keep her from seeing. I actually couldn't stand this. I didn't remember ever feeling this embarrassed. Ever.

Vince and Trixie shared a laugh while I regrouped.

"We'll actually be working on your problem right after detention today," Vince said to her.

"Good. I seriously cannot wait to get that succubus Mr. Kjelson off my back."

I turned to Vince with a raised eyebrow. He was always my go-to guy when people said something that didn't make sense. But to my surprise he just grinned and shrugged.

"What if he's still around?" Vince asked.

"He won't be," I said as we moved down the empty hallway toward Mr. Kjelson's classroom. "He's probably still at baseball tryouts in the gym, remember?"

We weren't old enough to have Mr. Kjelson as a teacher, but we'd found his classroom location on the school's website. I still was convinced that as a Cubs fan there was no way he could be as evil as Trixie made him out to be, but I'd also learned a long time ago never to trust someone's appearance entirely.

I took out the key I'd gotten from the janitor earlier that day. The janitor was a cool guy, even for an adult. We had an *understanding*, so he was always helpful when I needed access to something inside the school.

We were several feet from the classroom door when I was proved wrong about Kjelson not being there.

The door flew open, and Mr. Kjelson burst into the

hallway. Why wasn't he at practice?

My gut told me to dive for cover, but we were in a school hallway and there was nowhere to go. So I stood there, frozen, like a small critter about to get flattened all over a stretch of asphalt. Vince didn't move either.

But it didn't matter. Mr. Kjelson turned away from us immediately and barreled down the hallway in the opposite direction. His classroom door slowly eased back toward the frame and then right at the end slammed shut with a loud double thud.

Vince and I looked at each other.

"Why was he in such a hurry?" he said.

I shrugged and said, "Did you see what he was carrying?"

Vince nodded slowly.

We watched Mr. Kjelson reach the end of the hallway and turn left. He was walking so fast he was nearly running. In his left hand he held a large wire cage with at least two small furry animals inside. Neither appeared to be moving.

Vince and I turned to each other, nodded, and ran as quietly as we could after Mr. Kjelson. We needed to find out where he was going and what he was planning on doing to those animals.

We tracked him all the way out to the parking lot,

making sure to stay about twenty yards behind him at all times. I didn't know if that was too close or too far—Tyrell was my tailing expert; I wasn't used to fieldwork. A few times I thought for sure Mr. Kjelson would turn around and spot us and then that'd be it, but he never did. In fact, he was moving so fast that we had to jog to keep up.

When we got outside, Vince and I ducked behind a few bushes and watched as Kjelson went to his car. It was a small orange thing from at least the time of the dinosaurs, possibly older. But it did have a large Cubs sticker on the back. He opened the trunk and struggled to get the cage inside. The whole time he looked around so often that his head practically spun on his neck like a top. I'd never seen a teacher act so nervous before.

Then he got into his car and drove off.

Vince and I looked at each other from behind the bushes.

"Well, shall we head back to his classroom, then?" he asked.

"Um, yeah."

I was dying now more than ever to see what we could find.

The only person we saw in the halls on our way back was the janitor. He gave a brief nod of his head, and that was that. The janitor never asked questions. Which was perfect for me, because I didn't really like questions all that much.

Mr. Kjelson's classroom looked like any other science teacher's classroom. It had ten long, rectangular lab tables with shiny black tops and a small sink in the middle of each. The room was neat and orderly, and the teacher's desk was cleared of everything except for a computer and a little cup with pens and pencils inside of it.

"So what are we looking for?" Vince asked.

I shrugged. "Let's check out his desk."

He nodded. We moved around behind Mr. K.'s desk. I pulled at the top drawer, but it didn't budge. I tried a few of the others while Vince tried the drawers on the other side. None of them would open.

"Locked," I said.

"Where's Joe Blanton when you need him?"

I gave Vince a look.

"What?" he said. "Everyone knows that he can open locks with a single touch."

"Right, Vince, whatever. Joe Blanton couldn't open a lock if he had the key and the lock was already unlocked anyway."

"Numbers don't lie, Mac," Vince said, once again referring to Blanton's career 4.23 ERA or whatever pedestrian number it really was.

"We don't have time for this now," I said, but I also laughed. "What about that?" I pointed at the door behind Kjelson's desk. His office probably was behind it.

"Will that key get you into his office?" Vince asked.

"I don't know. I think so."

"Well, let's find out already."

I nodded, and we approached the door.

The key slid into the doorknob easily. As if it belonged. Behind the door I thought I heard desperate squeaking from several animals. Vince tensed next to me.

"Hurry up, Mac!"

I started turning the key, and then a voice behind us just about caused me to pee all over my favorite jeans.

"What exactly is going on here?"

I slid the key out and pocketed it as quickly as I could before turning around.

Mr. Kjelson stood a few feet away, leaning against a lab table with his arms crossed over his chest. His voice was clear and crisp, kind of like the sound of biting into an apple. He raised his eyebrows and tilted his head forward.

"Christian and Vince, were you trying to pick the lock to my office?" he asked.

"No, sorry, Coach. We were . . . I heard sounds coming from back there. They sounded like rats or something;

we were just trying to find out what they were," I said desperately. "What are you doing here anyway? Aren't you supposed to be at practice?"

Vince nodded.

"It ended early today. But shouldn't I be asking you the same thing?" he said. "You didn't even show up at all today."

Vince and I looked at each other.

"We were actually meaning to talk to you about that," I said. "See, we got detention; that's why we missed. And we'll be late tomorrow, too, also because of detention. But I swear we'll be there on time every time after that, Coach. And we'll play even harder. We'll make up for it."

"Fair enough." Mr. Kjelson nodded and examined us carefully. "You asked about noises coming from in there. Well, I put all the animals in my office every night because *somebody* has been stealing them," he said. "You guys know anything about that?"

It was more of an accusation than an actual question. But I decided to play along.

"Why would we want to steal lab animals?" I asked.

He shrugged. "You tell me."

I shrugged back.

"Okay, so if you aren't here for that, then can you possibly explain to me what you *are* doing in here *and* how you got in? I mean, you guys aren't even old enough to be in one of my classes, and you just said that you thought I was at practice, so it couldn't have been to come and tell me why you weren't there today. So where does that leave us?"

I glanced at Vince because I was fresh out of believable lies that could fit this situation. Plus, it's hard to think when you're panicking as much as I was right then. If Mr. Kjelson went to the Administration with this, and there was no reason not to, then Dr. George would really be on our cases. And he might even find out about my arrangement with the janitor. We'd be finished. Not only that, but this wasn't exactly helping our case to make the baseball team.

"The door was already open," Vince started.

Mr. Kjelson looked skeptical. "They lock automatically every time they close."

"It was ajar, not just unlocked," Vince countered.

Mr. Kjelson frowned.

Vince took a deep breath.

"Okay, here's what happened. We stayed after school because we got detention for trespassing in the kitchen earlier today. So Mac and I finished detention and we're wandering the halls, and you know, we're basically arguing about Joe Blanton and what matters more in baseball, numbers or intangibles, like always. Anyway, somehow the SMARTs came up because since Georgie, er, I mean Dr. George mentioned them yesterday, kids have been pretty concerned. Even teachers seem concerned. I heard from this one kid that his teacher, like, freaked out in class today, and after ranting about the SMARTs for several hours, he took off his shoes and socks and was pacing throughout the classroom talking about how the floor wasn't fit for his feet to walk on and also something about an alpaca, which I guess is some sort of rabid llama, that was trying to eat him in his dream last night or something.

"Anyways, so we were debating how good old Joe Blanton would do on such a test and I was saying that of course he would pass with flying colors. That he could pass the test in under two minutes even if you cut off his arms and only gave him a T-bone steak to write with. Basically, the only way he would fail is if he played for the Cubs, since the Cubs can't really win at anything. And Mac here was arguing that Blanton could never pass, not even if he was given the answer sheet while he took the test, not even if they let Joe write the test himself! Even then he'd score like negative fourteen percent, which is so bad that it isn't even mathematically possible.

"So this is where it gets really bizarre, right? So we're walking and talking, and then I swear I saw Joe

Blanton himself turn the corner and head this way. I kid you not. I could have sworn it was him. It was this tall, sort of portly dude with a nasty-awesome beard, and he was wearing pinstripes. So naturally we followed him. Except the hallway was empty, and then suddenly Christian here notices that your door is open, and we're like, 'Hey! Might as well take a peek and see if whatever teacher's classroom this is has any extra information on the SMARTs.' So we came on in with the idea of looking for SMART stuff, and then we heard some animal noises coming from your office and . . . here we are."

Vince panted beside me.

You see now why this guy was my right-hand man?

Mr. Kjelson didn't say a word. He just stood there, one arm still folded over his chest, the other reaching up and rubbing his chin lightly. He studied Vince. He studied us. His face was blank, as if he were in a trance.

The silence was practically exploding all around us like grenades it was so tense.

Then Mr. Kjelson did the last thing I ever expected him to do.

He laughed. He laughed until his face was red and tears were streaming down his face all over the floor, and he was slapping his leg over and over again. Okay, maybe it wasn't like that, but he did laugh pretty hard.

Vince and I glanced at each other, not sure what to do.

"Oh, that's too good, really," Mr. Kjelson said as he started calming down. "Okay, for that little bit of entertainment, I'm going to let you guys off with a warning. This time. But you may want to consider how serious this sort of thing is before doing it again. Because there are some teachers here who would probably try to suspend or even expel you for breaking into classrooms. Okay?"

"Really? We can just go?" I said.

"I can always reconsider if you'd like," Mr. Kjelson said.

"No, no. That's okay. Sorry for snooping, sir. We'll just go now, then."

Vince and I started inching toward the door.

I couldn't believe that we actually might get out of this scot-free. This wasn't exactly what I'd been expecting from Mr. Kjelson. It didn't match up at all with the story that the dark-haired girl had told us just an hour earlier. Something was up. Trixie had been lying to me for some reason—the question was why?

"So can you guys tell me what you were really doing here, or is it something I probably don't even want to know?" Mr. Kjelson said as we got to the door.

I turned around, shrugged, and pointed at Vince. "It

was like he said: we really were just curious about the SMARTs."

Mr. Kjelson nodded, and then a weird look came over his face, as if he'd hoped that part was actually a lie. Of course it was, but I don't think he knew that. I think he believed the part of the story that involved us looking for SMART information. Which seemed weird. . . . Was he just disappointed that we might have been trying to cheat? It felt like there was more to it than that.

"Okay, then, off with you. I'll see you guys tomorrow at tryouts," Kjelson said with a grin returning to his face. It was either the grin of the coolest guy alive or the grin of the devil himself. But I didn't stick around to get a second look. We basically sprinted the whole way through the halls and out the school's west door.

"That was close," Vince said once we were a good block from the school.

"Yeah, what was that all about? He was really cool about the whole thing."

Vince nodded. "No kidding. He was . . . I don't know. It's almost like he was *too* nice, though. No way any teacher is that cool of a person. No way."

"Exactly," I said. "Too nice. But . . . he is a Cubs fan."

Vince considered this. It was all just too confusing. We walked on and shook our heads for a while, letting our brains digest what had just happened.

"We need to look into this. We need to talk to some of his students and find out what's going on with this guy. And we possibly need to talk to Trixie again, too. There's something not right about this," I said.

"About Kjelson or about Trixie's story?"

"I don't know. Both, maybe. I mean, did you catch the weird way he reacted when we said we were just curious about the SMARTs? Either way, I know one thing: I intend to find out."

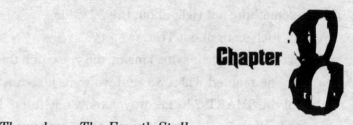

Thursday—The Fourth Stall

The next day during morning recess I interviewed a few kids from Kjelson's classes who Joe had rounded up for me. I had told him to pay each of them a couple dollars for their time. I'm normally the guy who got paid around here, but sometimes you've got to give a little to get something back.

The first kid was Kyle, a seventh grader who had Kjelson for General Biology sixth period. He sat across from me looking pretty relaxed.

"So what can you tell me about Mr. Kjelson?" I asked.

"He's my teacher."

"Right . . . I know that. Do you like him as a teacher?" I spoke slowly, as if talking to a dog.

"He's okay, I guess," Kyle said in a way that a dead fish might sound if it could talk.

This was what annoyed me most about some of the older kids. Talking to them was like talking to zombies. Actually it was worse. I'd rather have been talking to a zombie. At least then I could ask him interesting questions like "Do you ever miss being alive?" or "What do brains taste like?" Still, even from his one little comment I could tell that this kid hadn't had any real problems with Kjelson. Because most kids disliked their teachers, and they had no problems saying so. It's nature, like how a mother bird knows that it needs to chew the food for her babies and then spit it into their mouths.

"You ever see him freak out in class or yell at anybody?"

"I don't know," Kyle said. Except that he mashed it all together so it sounded like "I-uh-no."

"How could you not know? Have you seen him act that way or not?" I asked.

Kyle shifted in his chair and cleared his throat. "Can I go now?"

I sighed and made some notes in my Books. "Whatever."

Kyle got up and slid out of the bathroom, dragging his feet and groaning like zombies do in the movies. Despite Kyle's overall inability to speak clear English,

I could tell that Kjelson hadn't really done anything all that horrible in his class. Even someone like Kyle would have been able to say that much.

The next student was an eighth grader named Carissa who had Kjelson for Advanced Biology third hour.

"You have Mr. Kjelson, correct?'

"Yup."

"What can you tell me about him?"

"Like what?" she asked.

I tried to stay calm and still so as not to lead her one way or the other. I've often found that the way I ask things can change what people tell me. This is usually most true for the younger kids, but it can happen with anyone.

"What's he like, as a teacher?"

"Okay, well, he's a pretty nice guy. He's actually one of my favorite teachers. For some reason his class is never as boring as my other ones. He's always telling funny stories or doing cool things with the computer. I don't know. He just, like, makes class more fun than usual, I guess."

I nodded and tried to hide my frustration. Why wouldn't anyone spill the dirt on this guy? Maybe there was simply no dirt to spill?

"So you like him?"

She nodded.

"Has he ever yelled at anybody in class or done something unfair?"

"No, not really. I mean, one time he kicked this one kid named Justin out of class, but that's because Justin was being a real jerk. He was, like, making farting noises while Mr. K. tried to teach. As if he was still like ten or something. No offense."

I smiled and shook my head.

"Seriously, though," she continued. "Justin is so immature. We all hate him. But Mr. K. wasn't even all that mean, he just said, 'Justin, time for you to leave, please,' like that."

Only teachers who were well liked usually got called stuff like Mr. K. If a teacher who had a hard name were hated, then kids usually would just keep on mispronouncing the name because it really pissed off the teacher. Or they'd make up a mean way to say it instead.

"What about rumors? Have you heard stuff about Mr. K. being mean or anything like that?"

Carissa shrugged. "I guess one of my friends told me she heard he was a total jerk and that I'd hate him. But she didn't really know; she just heard that from someone else. I think he's nice, and so does everybody else in my class."

I nodded and let my breath out. I hadn't realized I'd been holding it. This whole mess probably couldn't get much more confusing. I bet this is what it felt like for a blind guy trying to do a Rubik's Cube.

"Okay, thanks, Carissa. One more thing. What about this girl, is she in Kjelson's class with you?"

I held out a picture of Trixie that I'd printed at home from the DVR camera in my office. Carissa looked at it, and then it happened. It was like one of those lightbulb moments you see in cartoons. Her face just lit up.

"Yeah, yeah. I mean, well, no, she's not in my class, but now that I see this, I do remember something. I saw this girl and Mr. K. arguing in the hall one day. It looked pretty heated, like it was about way more than what a normal student and teacher might be arguing about. I think I even heard him threaten to call her mom or something, which she seemed pretty upset over."

So finally there was something that backed up Trixie's story. Which of course only made me more confused than ever, since so far everything I'd found out had pointed toward her lying.

"Thanks," I said, and then paid Carissa a small fee for her time.

She smiled, nodded, and left.

It was more of the same from other kids I interviewed that day. Some had nothing bad to report about

Mr. Kjelson. Actually, most of them really seemed to like the guy as a teacher. But one other kid also said he saw a pretty tense exchange between Trixie and Mr. Kjelson in the hall one day. And maybe the most confusing part of all was that none of the kids I'd interviewed that day had said that Trixie was in Kjelson's class during the same hour as they were.

Finding Tyrell was getting harder these days. He'd told me the week before that'd he'd been honing his concealment skills. Apparently he'd just gotten a new book called *Self-Camouflaging: The Art of Being Invisible*. And it must've been a pretty good book because it took me the better part of lunch period that day to find the kid.

Or I guess he found me, if you want to get technical.

I was down the hill near the new playground that the school had installed last year between the football field and the Shed. It was the kind with big plastic, interconnected red, yellow, and blue slides with platforms and clear plastic bubble windows. Not many kids used this playground; most of them still hung out up the hill near all the old metal, dangerous stuff: the slides so slick that you got a face full of gravel at the end, the teeter-totters so high and heavy that a cherry bump felt like a kick in the butt from a professional soccer player, the two giant truck tires that reeked of toxic rubber and broken limbs, the old chain-link swings that went so high you could see the roof of the school, and, last but not least, the caged dome, which was perfect for high climbing, long falls, and battle royale cage-match wrestling tournaments and fights. One of the older kids had named it Thunderdome.

That's why I thought I might find Tyrell by the new playground. It was usually deserted. Every once in a while a group of first graders might head down and play on the plastic behemoth, but normally it just sat there empty and expensive looking.

I looked up all the slides and in every platform fort area on the big plastic complex. But it was empty. I jumped down into the sand and headed back toward the hill, utterly perplexed as to where Tyrell could be. I'd already checked all his usual places.

I was almost at the end of the huge sandbox housing the whole new playground system when a hand grabbed my ankle. I screamed and jumped high enough to dunk on a regulation basketball hoop.

"Shh, Mac, it's just me. Calm down," the sand said.

But sand can't talk. At least not usually.

"What?" I said, backing away slowly.

Then Tyrell sat up out of nowhere and sand fell all around him. He had been lying in the sandbox the entire time. I'd probably even stepped on him and didn't notice.

"How?" is all I could really manage to say.

Tyrell stood up and brushed the loose sand off of his clothes. Then I saw "how." He was wearing sand-colored sweatpants and a matching sweatshirt with the hood up. The clothes were still caked in sand, and that's when I realized that he had somehow glued sand all over the sweat suit. His shoes were also caked in sand. A small sand-colored straw stuck out of his mouth.

He reached a sand arm up, removed the straw, and pulled down his hood.

"What's up, Mac? Need help with something?"

"That's some outfit," I said, walking back into the sandbox.

He shrugged and grinned at me. The kid was beyond unreal when it came to spying. He took his craft seriously, and it showed time and again with his amazing results. There was a good reason he was the highest-paid person on my payroll.

"Actually I do need your help," I said, "finding out some stuff about a girl."

"Oh yeah? What kind of stuff?" he asked, raising his eyebrows.

"It's not like that, Tyrell. I basically just need to know her name, who she hangs out with, after-school activities she's in. You know, the usual."

"The Works, then?"

I nodded. "Why do girls lie so much, Tyrell?"

Tyrell shrugged a single shoulder and then smiled. "We *all* lie, Mac."

He was right. I'd done my fair share of lying. But lying to teachers and adults was one thing. Lying to your fellow students was entirely different. Especially when you're lying to probably the one guy in the whole school who can solve your problem.

"The usual fee okay?" I asked.

Tyrell nodded.

"I also would like you to see if you can find out if Mr. Kjelson is up to anything suspicious. I don't think he is, but maybe you could just confirm that for me."

"Hey, that's why I'm here," he said.

"I know, exactly, *and* I may have even more for you when you're done with these two assignments. I need to know more about the SMARTs. I mean, kids seem to be getting more worried about them every day, and even the teachers are acting weird. So I kind of want to make sure they're not going to be a problem. Also, I may even need more help after that, so maybe take it easy on the whole invisible thing for a few days?"

"Sure thing, Mac. I'll be stopping by sometime soon with that info."

"Okay, thanks, buddy."

I gave him a salute before heading back toward the school. That's another thing that I loved about Tyrell: not only was he good at what he did, but he was fast, too. I couldn't say either of those things about too many kids these days.

Chapter 9

Thursday—The School Hallway

After school, on our way to detention, Vince hit me right in the face with a hard one. Not a fist punch, just a trivia question, but they felt close to the same sometimes.

"Which team did the Cubs beat during their first-ever game at Wrigley Field in 1916?" he asked.

I shook my head and did a little stomp as if I was frustrated. I saw Vince's grin spread. He was sure he had me now.

"That's not even fair, Vince. You looked that up earlier, didn't you? Remember, you can't Google questions to make them super hard. The question has to be something you already knew for at least a few months."

"I knew this, Mac. Come on, what do you take me for, a cheater?"

I shook my head and then started laughing. I couldn't help it. He just looked so proud of himself. When he realized what I was laughing about, his smile faded a little.

"That's not funny, Mac. I really thought I had you."

"Well, sorry, but the answer is the Cincinnati Reds, seven to six in eleven innings."

"Well done, sir," Vince said clapping loud and slow to show me he was being sarcastic.

We stifled our laughs as we entered Mr. Daniels's room. We handed him our detention slips and nodded when he gave his usual spiel about the difference between social hour (whatever that is) and detention. Then we faced the desks, and I spotted her immediately. Despite her dark hair she just had a way of being noticed. She stuck out. But in a good way, I thought.

I nudged Vince, and he nodded. We sat on either side of Trixie.

"Kjelson got you again, huh?" I said as we sat down.

She snorted. "No thanks to you."

"Well, you see, I actually wanted to talk to you about that. I *have* been working on your so-called problem. And I'm not really sure what to think about it."

"What does *that* mean?" she asked.

I could practically hear her rattle blurring into action.

"What do you think it means?" I asked.

Any trace of her sly grin could no longer be seen. Her neon eyes narrowed, and I thought she was about to telepathically explode my head all over our fellow detainees like in this old Canadian movie called *Scanners* that Vince made me watch with him once. Thankfully Mr. Daniels broke her concentration and spared me my head.

"Quiet down! This is detention not social hour!"

"Look," Vince said quietly, placing one hand between the dark-haired girl and me. "What Mac means to say is that your story isn't exactly adding up."

"What do you mean 'adding up'? This isn't a math equation or anything; it's just some jerk of a teacher!"

She said it so loudly that she actually stirred Mr. Daniels out of his normal clockwork scolding.

"Hey, what did I just say? Quiet down!" he said, looking right at us. Then he turned his attention back to his computer.

We gave him a few minutes to settle back into whatever he was doing at his computer and then I spoke in a low whisper.

"What we mean is that Mr. Kjelson doesn't seem all that bad. I've gone to every student I can find who has this guy as a teacher, and they all like him. In fact most kids seem to think he's one of the best teachers they've ever had! So how can I fix the problem when there's really no problem to fix?"

I conveniently left out the part about hearing from several sources that she'd had a run-in with Kjelson in the hallway because, even with that backing her story, I still got the feeling she was lying to me in some way. So I wanted to test her.

"Don't be such a fool, Mac," she said softly.

"What?"

"Are you really that much of an idiot?" she asked with seemingly genuine surprise that embarrassed me a little bit. "He's charming you just like everybody else. He's like a Jedi: it's not hard for him to fool the weak-minded. I guess I thought you'd be more perceptive than that but obviously not. He's got you right where he wants you, along with all the other suckers around here. Mr. Kjelson *is* evil. I told you that. He's the worst kind of evil because you won't even realize it until it's too late. That's why he only picks on me. I'm probably the only one here who's got him figured out."

I leaned back in my chair and stared into her eyes. For the first time they actually looked afraid and not like a predator's. I didn't really know what to say. What if she was right? Could he have us all fooled? I had been wrong before. In fact I'd misjudged Fred so horribly just a few months ago that it had almost ended up costing me everything. Besides, Vince and I had seen Kjelson practically sprinting from the school with a cage full of possibly dead animals. That had to mean *something*. We had even caught him in a flat-out lie—he had told us someone else was stealing the animals. Teachers lie all the time, of course, but not usually about stuff like that. And there was the detail that a few kids had somewhat corroborated her story.

"But if he has everybody fooled, what can I do?" I asked.

"I don't know. That's why I came to you! Aren't you supposed to be the big genius? The big-shot problem solver? You're not really as advertised, you know."

"Hey, I just have to do my research, that's all."

"Well, if you really don't believe me, why don't you just ask him about me? See if you can see through his lies then. My real name is Hannah Carol. Ask him about me."

I nodded. "Okay, we will."

"We'll figure it out, okay?" Vince added. "I promise. It's like my grandma always says, 'It ain't over until somebody gets eaten alive by a swarm of flying lamp shades.'"

His grandma did say that, too. I had heard her say it once after we lost a baseball game that summer. Vince's whole family had groaned because some big-city team had seriously killed us by the mercy rule, but Vince had smiled, proud of his grandma's assessment of our recently received butt kicking.

Hannah was silent for some time. Then she exploded into the loudest laughter I'd heard in a while in detention. She laughed so loud that even Mr. Daniels couldn't ignore it. He stood up and started shouting.

"Quiet down! This is detention! I said, *quiet*!"

She just kept on laughing, and Mr. Daniels's normally pale face filled with red, as if somebody had just opened his skull and poured in a whole pitcher of tomato juice.

"Stop that!" he shouted.

But now everybody else was laughing, too, not just Hannah. Except they weren't laughing at Vince's line; they were laughing at Mr. Daniels. And also just because. Kids know when a situation gets out of the teacher's control, and they will seize that opportunity every time. Especially the detention kids.

We were all laughing now, and Daniels looked like he was on the verge of a heart attack. His face was practically bleeding out of every pore, he was so red, and he was pounding on his desk.

"Quiet! Quiet! Quiet! *This is detention not social hour!*"

We just kept laughing, and for a moment I almost forgot about how confused I was over whether Mr. Kjelson was good or bad and whether the dark-haired girl was lying to me or not.

After detention we rushed to baseball practice as quickly as we could. We were late due to detention. We apologized, even though Mr. K. had known we'd be late, and took our spots in the lines.

That day we worked on upping the velocity on the pitchers' fastballs and also started working on some breaking pitches. I think even in the limited bit of time that Mr. Kjelson watched Vince, Vince pretty much blew away the coach with his circle change and a knuckle-ball he'd been working on lately. In fact Vince blew away everybody. His catchers even had a hard time following his pitches through their sharp and seemingly random breaks. I started to realize that there may be a good chance that only one of us would make the team and it wouldn't be me. The only thing I had going for me was that I was the only one who didn't miss a single one of Vince's pitches, because I was so used to catching him.

After practice ended, Kjelson called Vince and me aside. "You played well today. Definitely made up for missing some time the past few days."

I glanced at Vince, unsure of what to say. Vince just shrugged and then mumbled a thank-you. He's never been good at taking compliments.

"So you two are Cubs fans, right?" he asked, changing the subject.

"Hey, is the pope Gouda?" I asked. I knew that that saying is supposed to go "Is the Pope Catholic?" but I liked Vince's grandma's version better.

Kjelson gave me a look and then chuckled. "I'll take that as a yes. What did you guys think about their trade yesterday?"

Vince and I spoke simultaneously, "It stinks!"

Coach Kjelson laughed and nodded. "I thought so, too. How could they trade away their best prospect for an aging forty-year-old slugger with arthritis and a .213 average last season? Makes no sense."

Vince and I shook our heads solemnly.

"The curse," I said.

"The curse," Kjelson agreed with a nod. "Well, you never know. Maybe it will all work out this year somehow."

A cold silence followed, and then we all burst out laughing. We all knew there was little chance of that happening. But what was so funny was that we also knew that all three of us were still secretly hoping that the Cubs would find a way to win, just like we all did every year. It really was a painful thing being a true Cubs fan, going through a routine, slow and regular heart smashing year after year.

I decided now was as good a time as any to follow up on Hannah's, aka Trixie's, suggested authenticity check.

"So, Mr. Kjelson, what can you tell me about a Hannah Carol?"

He was taken aback for a moment, more so, it seemed, than if I'd asked him about some other random student. He furrowed his brow, and his smile disappeared, and for the second time I wondered if I was getting a glimpse of that other side to Mr. Kjelson that Hannah swore existed and that nobody else could see.

"Why do you ask?"

I shrugged. "Just curious, I guess. I heard some things, that's all."

Now his eyes narrowed into black darts that could have passed right through a sheet of stainless steel. "What do you mean? What have you heard?"

He looked truly concerned, as if some secret was in danger of getting out. I didn't know where to go from here. Suddenly I got the impression that this line of questioning was dangerous, that I shouldn't have asked at all. But then Vince saved me from having to get myself out of it, as was usual.

"Oh hey, my mom's waiting for us," he said. "We better go."

"See ya, Coach Kjelson," I said.

As we left the gym, I looked back and saw Kjelson

still staring at me darkly.

In his mom's car Vince and I exchanged looks that suggested he was thinking the exact same thing. I was sort of feeling pretty grateful right then that the next practice wasn't until Tuesday.

Chapter 10

Friday—School Hallway

Friday morning at early recess Vince and I stopped by Tony Adrian's locker to check on the traps we'd set earlier that week. Tony was there waiting for us, looking more nervous and fidgety than usual.

"There's more in there. I can tell already," he said. "I can feel it."

Vince and I exchanged a glance. "Let's have a look," Vince said.

Tony put in his locker combination and then stepped aside. Vince opened the locker door and I peered inside.

Tony was right: there were more of the small droppings piled in the bottom of the locker. They were sitting right in the middle of our trap.

But the trap was empty.

"Is that even possible?" I said.

Vince shook his head. "I don't see how. There's no way an animal could get in here, take a deuce, and then leave without being caught in that trap. No way."

"What could that mean, then? Is it an invisible rat?"

"Unless we're dealing with the Joe Blanton of rodents here, I don't see how it's possible that an animal left these at all."

"Which means someone else—a kid—is putting them here?"

We both looked at Tony. He held up his impossibly clean hands and said, "Hey, don't look at me. I'd rather get ten cavities filled than even look at that stuff."

"Maybe it's a prank, like someone knows Tony is a clean freak. No offense," Vince said.

Tony shrugged, accepting that he was in fact a neat freak.

"Maybe," I said, "but that doesn't explain why so many other kids have complained to us about the same problem. And they're kids from all different grades so it seems to be totally random."

Vince shook his head. It was hard to stump Vince, so this really was somewhat of a mystery. "What about the Beagle?"

I nodded. "Yeah, let's do that."

Luckily we had come prepared. Vince took out a pair of plastic gloves and a plastic sandwich baggie. He carefully put some of the droppings into the bag, and then we double-bagged them and threw those bags into a brown paper bag. Hey, we weren't taking any chances. Vince disposed of his gloves and wandered off to find a bathroom to wash his hands.

"We'll figure this out eventually," I said. "And we'll make sure to send the Hutt by later to finish the cleaning."

Tony nodded his head.

At lunch that day Jonah came back to the East Wing bathroom. This time he seemed much calmer than he had on his first visit. But he still insisted on running in place while in my office. I didn't argue. I figured there was really no point with health psychos like Jonah.

"So I guess I probably don't need your help anymore," he said.

"What do you mean?" I asked.

"Well, Dr. George apparently, you know, he was, like, brought in to clean up our school since it's been, like, falling apart, and one of the first things he did was to get our school a proper menu. I went to see him, and he was horrified at what we were being served. He called it a tragedy and said that America was tubby enough already or something like that. Anyway, thanks, Mac, but yesterday the lunch was great. We had boiled chicken, steamed broccoli, and plain brown rice."

I thought that lunch sounded way worse than what they had been serving, but even beyond that was the fact that George had now stolen a customer from me. I didn't like this at all. He was going to bleed me dry of my paying customers if he kept this up.

"So can I, like, get a refund, then?" Jonah asked while still jogging in place.

"Definitely," I said as I put the Tom Petty cashbox on my desk. I hated giving out refunds, but it was the right thing to do. I mean, technically someone else had solved his problem before I could.

I counted out his money and then made some notes in my Books before handing the cash to him.

"Sorry I couldn't be more help," I said.

He shrugged. "It's all the same to me. I'm just happy I'm not going to be fed Type Two on a plate anymore."

I wasn't sure exactly what he meant by that, but if he was happy with everything, then I guess I had to be, too. Except I wasn't. At this rate we were going to lose money this month instead of making record profits like it had looked like we would at the beginning of the week.

Near the end of lunch we closed the office so Vince and I could take the sample from Tony's locker to the

Beagle for analysis. The Beagle still owed me a favor for when I'd helped him obtain uranium for some science project he was doing earlier in the year. Don't even ask how I got that uranium. If I told you, I might have to kill you.

The Beagle was this fifth grader who was obsessed with science and especially animal science. He loved animals so much that he was that kid who, back in second grade, would bring in a different pet every week for show-and-tell. He never even had to repeat, he owned so many. And basically in any conversation you ever had with him or to anything at all you could say to him, he'd respond with some crazy pet story. It's like the only way he knew to communicate—with stories about his pets. Also, one time in third grade I saw him outside walking his pet hamster on a custom miniature leash. I figured if anybody could lead us to the origins of the locker poop, it was the Beagle.

We found him in one of the science labs. I'd heard from Ears, my go-to informant, that the Beagle spent his lunch and recess time in there. He was hunched over one of the black lab tables working furiously on something and saying stuff like, "Yes! Perfect! That's just what this needed! Ha. Haha. Hahahaha!" and on and on like that.

We approached where he was sitting with his back

to us. Then suddenly, without turning around, he said, "I've been expecting you."

Vince and I stopped and looked at each other,

"How did you know we were here?" I asked.

The Beagle spun on his stool and faced us. He was still blocking whatever it was he was working on from our view, and I figured that was probably for the better. Part of me didn't really even want to know.

"First I heard you come in," he said. "Then I smelled who you were when you approached."

He twitched his long nose. He wore thin small glasses, and he had pretty big ears and an oblong head with just a small tuft of hair on top, as if he had problems growing any more hair than that.

"Why were you expecting us?" Vince asked.

"Well, I've been hearing things about feces being found in several kids' lockers, and I figured it would be only a matter of time before you came to me for help. I still owe you a favor after all, do I not?"

I tilted my head toward him. I had to hand it to this kid—he was pretty sharp. I just hoped he knew animals as well as we all thought he did.

"Well, then, have you brought me a sample?" he asked.

"Actually, we did," I said.

Vince handed him the brown paper bag. The Beagle smiled and opened it and motioned for us to join him at a different lab table across the room. I tried to sneak a peek at whatever it was he had been working on, but he tossed a white sheet over it before joining us at the new lab table.

The Beagle removed the plastic bags and then carefully opened them. He removed the droppings by pouring them gently into a shallow plastic cylinder. Then he removed a pair of tweezers from his pocket and started prodding at the samples.

"Hmm," he said. "I see. Yes, very interesting."

"What is it?" I asked.

He didn't answer me directly but instead kept poking and muttering things to himself like, "Yes, indeed," and "How about that," and "Just as I suspected." Then he turned to face us.

"Well, you've definitely got feces from a *Cricetus cricetus* here. Also some from a *Meriones unguiculatus*, and even a *Cavia porcellus*. It's a veritable pantheon of common captive critter crap you've brought me."

"One more time in words I can understand," I said. Experts: you have to love how they use their own jargon and technical terms as if we normal people would understand them. It's like if I understood any of that, then why would I be coming to you for your expertise?

"Well, these originated from three different animals:

a hamster, a gerbil, and a guinea pig."

Now that just didn't make any sense at all.

"You're sure?" I asked.

"Definitely. Here, let me show you. . . ." He picked up a sample with his tweezers.

"No, no, that's okay. I'm sure you know what you're doing. Thanks a bunch. Consider that favor repaid."

"Great. Thanks, Mac," he said.

As Vince and I walked back to our office, we didn't have much to say for the first several minutes. It was hard to wrap our heads around what the Beagle's information meant exactly.

"So this is like that one time Joe Blanton struck out twenty-eight batters in six innings while he was still driving to the stadium because he was running late," Vince finally said.

Normally I'd have laughed right then, but at the moment I was still too confused to offer much more than a nod.

"I guess this means that someone has to be planting the poop in kids' lockers," I said. "There's no way that all three of those animals are just roaming around together and pooping in a pack like some sort of odd gang of misfit lab animals."

"I know, but who could it be? And why?"

"Well, we did see Mr. Kjelson sneaking around suspiciously after hours with cages of rodents," I said.

Vince tilted his head and said, "Yeah, that's true, plus he has access to all of the science lab animals. But what could his motive possibly be?"

We both shook our heads just then, frustrated with the inexplicable nature of our recent discovery.

Chapter 11

Monday—Gymnasium

Monday and Wednesday mornings are when my regular class goes to the gymnasium for physical education class. On that particular Monday I saw firsthand what those jocks had come to me complaining about the week before.

We got there, changed clothes in the locker room, and then headed out to the gym, where we found our gym teacher, Mr. Fields. He was short and very muscular. But he was almost too muscular for how short he was because, instead of looking like a normal tough guy or an action-movie star, he mostly just looked like a troll on steroids. He always wore these really short gym shorts that you'd have had to pay me a ton of money to wear in public. And he always had his whistle either hanging from his thick neck or tucked into his mouth somewhere under his huge mustache. His mustache was so huge that it seemed to have a life of its own. All the students called it "The 'Stache." One kid even swore that it talked to him once. He said it made fun of his own measly attempt at a mustache. But what did the 'Stache expect? The kid was only an eighth grader.

Mr. Fields was a typical gym teacher, which meant basically all you could ever count on him for was yelling at kids to take showers, screaming the word "hustle" repeatedly, and blowing his whistle at random moments. I sometimes wondered if gym teachers became gym teachers because a school gym was really the only place where they could just be themselves without being thought of as complete weirdos.

On that Monday Mr. Fields was standing next to another gym teacher, Mrs. Dumas. She was known around school for always wearing these bright orange-and-pink psychedelic spandex pants with ugly, fluorescent track jackets. It was hilarious how much she loved neon colors and spandex.

But it wasn't funny now because with her was a class of older kids. Not just older kids: older girls. I didn't like at all where this was headed.

"Gentlemen," Mr. Fields yelled—he always called

us gentlemen—"today, you are going to learn how to dance!"

I wasn't sure why that was worth shouting about, but he was a gym teacher: they were always shouting about something. I wondered if gym teachers were like that at home, too. I could just see Mr. Fields at the dinner table with his family. He'd blow his shrill whistle and then scream, "Pass me the peas!" Then as his wife's shaking hands passed the bowl of peas, he'd blow his whistle again and scream, "Hustle, hustle, hustle!" and cause her to drop the bowl. Then he'd get really mad and shout, "Okay, no slacking allowed here! Drop and give me fifteen push-ups, Mrs. Fields!" She'd probably do the push-ups, too, after which Mr. Fields would blow his whistle yet again and say, "Okay, hit the showers!"

Anyway, the class groaned after Mr. Fields's announcement.

"But dancing is for sissies," one of my classmates whined.

Mr. Fields blew his whistle and then approached the kid who'd made the comment. He got right in the kid's face, since Mr. Fields was short enough that he really didn't have to bend over to do it.

"What was that, Mr. Schmidt?" Mr. Fields yelled, spraying the kid's face with spit and mustache. Even the 'Stache looked angry.

The kid shook his head.

"That's what I thought," Mr. Fields said, turning to address us all again. "Dancing is not for sissies. Cheerleading is for sissies, marching band is for sissies, theater is for sissies, swimming is for sissies. *Dancing* . . . is for men. Dancing is the way to win that girl you've got your eye on. Does that sound like a sissy pursuit to you?"

Nobody answered, and the gym was dead silent. It felt pretty uncomfortable. Some kid coughed, and Mr. Fields took a breath, but Mrs. Dumas spoke before he could.

"Well, Mr. Fields, why don't we dive right in, yes?"

He looked at her as if he'd forgotten she was there, and then he nodded and blew his whistle. They paired us up with the older girls so they could teach us individually. And I just about hit the floor when I saw who my partner was.

"Well, hi there, Mac," Hannah said with a grin so sweet that it was likely just meant to numb me so I couldn't run.

"Oh, hey, Hannah," I said.

She giggled. "Are you ready to learn the jitterbug?" she asked.

I rolled my eyes, and she giggled again. I'd never seen her act so nice before. It was alarming and kind of pleasant at the same time. I didn't know what to make of it.

"Here, you start by putting your left foot here." She

pointed at a place on the floor.

I did as she told me. She gave me another series of directions, and I had to say, whatever that jitterbug thing was, man, was it lame. And hard. I kept tripping myself. And tripping Hannah, which I thought for sure would get me in trouble, but she actually didn't seem to mind. She just giggled. So at one point I figured I might as well show her that I could be funny, too. It wasn't just Vince who could get a laugh around here.

"Hey, this is kind of like my godfather Bruce always says, 'If you're awake, then it ain't ever too early to start hailing Mary,' " I said.

My godfather did say that, too. I wasn't quite sure what he meant by it, but whenever he said it, my parents would groan and exchange looks. I figured that was just as funny as the things Vince's grandma sometimes said.

Hannah gave me a funny look, and then she snorted. "What?"

"Oh, um, never mind," I said quickly. I guessed my godfather wasn't quite as funny as Vince's grandma after all.

"No, seriously, Mac. What did you mean by that? Was that supposed to be funny?" she asked. That snakelike glint was back in her eyes, and I suddenly wished I'd just kept my mouth shut.

I shook my head.

She could have kept teasing me, but instead she just chuckled. "Mac, don't try so hard."

"What do you mean?" I asked. "This jitterbug thing isn't easy."

Hannah grinned at me and then rolled her eyes.

I didn't know what to do next so I just smiled and nodded. "Okay then, Ms. Von Parkway—or Ms. Carol—after you." Then I led her in another round of the lame jitterbug that ended in us crashing into the kids next to us, which started a domino effect of falling dancing couples. It ended with Mr. Fields blowing his whistle over and over as if that could somehow stop kids from falling. Hannah and I could barely hold in our laughter.

We did the jitterbug for the rest of class, and I didn't think I'd ever seen so many kids hit the ground. We were all bruised and limping and whining by the time class was over. If it hadn't been for Hannah, that would have been the worst gym class in history.

Gym class that day taught me three things: 1) Maybe Hannah wasn't so bad after all; 2) Gym class had become a joke. Dancing? Since when do middle schoolers do dancing in gym class?; and 3) Gym teachers are insane. What kind of sadistic psychopath would pair up sixth-grade boys with eighth-grade girls? The school was lucky that nobody got puked on or seriously injured.

Chapter 12

Monday—The Fourth Stall

Business was steady at early recess that day just as it had been on Friday. And the majority of kids were coming to me about the SMARTs. It seemed that more and more kids were hearing rumors about both how hard they were and how important it was to pass them. One kid told me he'd even heard that if you failed them, you could get held back a year instantly, just like that, no matter what your grades were.

I now had offers on the table from over two dozen kids telling me that if I could make sure they passed, they'd pay me big bucks. There certainly seemed to be a lucrative side to these SMARTs, but messing with standardized tests was risky; it was something I'd never tried before. So I needed to know more about the SMARTs before I seriously considered all of the kids' offers.

Which is why it was awesome that near the end of early recess Tyrell came to my office with information for me, just like he'd said he would. I was hoping he'd at least help me get closer to putting the whole Mr. Kjelson mystery behind me, if not give me a lead on the SMARTs. Turns out those would be the least of my worries that day, but I'll get into that more in a bit.

"So what do you have for me?" I asked Tyrell after he sat down across from me in the fourth stall from the high window.

"Pretty much everything on the girl. The teacher was a little tougher, but I got some stuff on him, too, as well as the SMARTs."

"Let's have it," I said. He handed me a professional-looking dossier complete with vital statistics and surveillance photos.

According to Tyrell, Hannah Carol hung out mostly with seventh and eighth graders since she'd started about halfway through the school year. She had a lot of friends, but as far as Tyrell could tell, she didn't really belong to any one certain group or clique. The only after-school activity she participated in was the Theater Production Team/Audio Visual Club. They basically did everything that required lighting or sound effects, such as plays, assemblies, and eighth-grade graduations, and some kids in the club even helped out with sound equipment for school dances, PTA meetings, and any school meetings open to the public.

Both Tyrell and I thought it was pretty strange that *that* was the one extracurricular activity she was into, as it was normally designated for geeky kids. And Hannah didn't really strike me as the geeky type, despite her Star Wars reference the week before. But at the same time the girl could be so perplexing that her one strange activity actually made sense a little bit. She was pretty weird. Other than that Tyrell said he'd found out nothing too out of the ordinary for Hannah.

"What about Mr. Kjelson?" I asked.

"He checked out okay, actually. As far as I can tell, there's nothing too unusual going on with him. I mean, I saw him leaving school with some lab animals yesterday just like you guys did, but that doesn't prove much of anything—maybe they're his and he just brings them to class each day? I also saw him yesterday with a big packet of documents that had SMART stamped all over them, but that could mean a lot of things."

So there *was* a connection between Kjelson and the SMARTs. But what exactly was it? Was he just another teacher who would administer them later this week? Or was it more than that? This bit of news was especially interesting considering the weird look on his face when I'd brought up the tests the week before in his class-room.

"I couldn't find a whole lot else because he's so new here. He started teaching here just after the school year started. I did discover that he taught at Oaks Crossing private school last year. While there he won teacher of the year twice."

"Oaks Crossing . . ." I said, and looked through my Books. That was supposedly where his son went to school, according to Hannah. It seemed odd to me that he'd transfer away from his son, since Oaks Crossing is almost twenty miles from here. "So he transferred away from where his son goes to school? Any way you might be able to find out why?"

"Wait a second, Mac. Who said anything about a son?"

"Well, that's the whole reason I'm even looking into this. Apparently Hannah dated Kjelson's son for a while and it caused problems and blah, blah, blah." But it was already dawning on me where this was headed.

"Mac, Mr. Kjelson doesn't have a son," Tyrell said.

I heard Vince shuffle his feet outside the stall. He must have heard Tyrell and was likely trying to keep from falling over from shock. Were I not sitting down, I'd surely have been on the floor right then myself.

"What?"

"I'm sorry, Mac, but it's pretty solid. I found this biography thing he wrote and posted to the school website when he got hired. He doesn't mention a son in it at all, and he goes on and on about everything else in his life, so why would he not mention a son?"

I nodded.

So Hannah had been lying to me all along, it seemed, at least about one thing. And just when I was actually starting to like her. But why? What did Mr. Kjelson have against her, then, if anything? Why did she even make up a story about Bryce at all? Everybody knows that I don't ask questions that don't need answering. If she'd just said, "Hey, this teacher is a jerk to me," that would have been enough. I'd thought I couldn't get more lost in this problem, but now I really felt helpless. Plus, if Kjelson was such a great guy and teacher as he seemed to be, then why was Hannah constantly in detention? Who was putting her there? What explanation could there be for the heated exchange they'd supposedly had in the hallway?

"What about the SMARTs?" I asked, eager to move on to a subject less confusing than girls.

"Well, it seems like they're a pretty big deal," Tyrell said.

I nodded. I was beginning to suspect as much with

the way teachers and kids had been acting lately. The question was how big of a deal were they?

"They're, like, a really, really big deal, Mac. I did a little research, and I found out that another school in the southern part of the state got closed down in the middle of the year because of how poorly they did on the SMARTs. They're that huge."

That was pretty huge. I'd never heard of such a thing.

"And here's the thing," Tyrell continued, "the tests are pretty hard. That school that failed, well, their other standardized test scores in recent years have been pretty similar to those at our school, Mac. So if they could fail, then potentially so could we."

I tried to envision my school, our school, closing down overnight in the middle of the school year. The thought seemed ridiculous to me but also scary in a weird way. I mean, isn't that every kid's dream? For his school just to be shut down one day? Then why did the thought bother me so much? Either way, I decided we definitely could not just ignore this SMART thing coming up. If all of the kids offering me money weren't enough for me to take action, the possibility that my school and business could be shut down certainly was.

"Okay, Tyrell, I need you to get everything you can for me on this test. What day we're taking it, what's the procedure, the format, everything. You think you could get all that within a day or two?"

He breathed in sharply but then grinned. "Well, it won't be easy, and therefore it won't be cheap. But if anyone can do it, then I'm going to."

I nodded. That was vintage Tyrell, confident to a fault, if he wasn't too good to have faults. "Okay, let's outline a payment schedule here—" I wasn't able to finish because I heard Fred calling my name from the first stall.

"Mac! He's coming this way. Dr. George is coming down here right now!"

This was good news and bad news. The good news was that the expensive investment in those security cameras was actually paying off. The bad news was, obviously, that we were all screwed.

Chapter 13

Monday—The Fourth Stall

My first reaction was that perhaps Fred was wrong, that Dr. George was headed this way for some other reason. Then I came to my senses and realized just what would happen if Dr. George noticed a giant line of kids outside a supposedly closed bathroom and then found me in there with a desk in a stall, my Books, and a cashbox containing a few hundred dollars: my business would be no more.

I heard what sounded like a billion footsteps as the kids in line ran for their lives. Then the door to the bathroom burst open, and I heard Joe yell, "Mac, Dr. George is coming. What should we do?"

I turned to tell Tyrell to take off, but he was no longer

there. All that sat across from me in the small plastic chair was air and some dust particles. Even now, in a time of life-shattering chaos, I had to take half a second to admire the kid.

I stepped out of my office and into the bathroom. The three panicked faces of Joe, Fred, and Vince stared at me.

"Guys, we've been over this," I said. "Initiate Operation Tuxedo Bacon."

Operation Tuxedo Bacon was a procedure we'd put in place way back when we'd first adopted this bathroom as my office. It was designed for this exact situation: What would we do if someone from the Administration ever came down this way? If you can believe it, it had yet to happen. The Suits don't often venture too far from their offices, especially not all the way down here to the East Wing. There was nothing down here but this old bathroom and a few classrooms that were shut down years ago due to asbestos and had never been used again since the removal.

Now it was time to see if Operation T.B. actually worked.

Joe dove inside my office and placed the three plastic chairs on top of the desk. Then he lifted the whole thing off the ground and carried it to the next stall over. He sat on the toilet with the small desk and chairs balanced on his lap and then shut the stall's door. This part of the plan was key, as only Joe's feet could be seen under the stall, thereby eliminating all traces of the desk and chairs. It never would have worked if Joe were a normal-sized kid, because most normal-sized kids would have buckled under the pressure of a desk and three chairs. Luckily for us he was practically the size of a small truck.

While Joe did this, Vince ran out to the hallway to intercept Dr. George and distract him with questions or stories of some sort. Vince could spin stuff off like nobody's business, so I trusted he'd buy us enough time to get everything concealed.

Meanwhile Fred stood there looking like a Tasered criminal while I scrambled to get all my Books and locked cashbox stored in the trash can, where I normally stored them each night after school before we all went home. Fred had no duties because he hadn't been around when we came up with Operation T.B.

I grabbed the DVRs out of the first stall and shoved them into his hands. They were almost too much for him to carry, but he held on. "Fred, just go!" I whispered.

He nodded and dashed out the door.

I finished stashing all of our Books and the cashbox and then got out my key to the bathroom. Ideally the plan was for me to make it out quickly enough to lock the bathroom door from the outside so any approaching

Suits wouldn't be able to get in right away. The janitor had provided us with a pretty authentic-looking "Out of Order for Health Code Reasons" sign that would explain why the bathroom was locked.

I could hear voices already, so I knew I didn't have time for the health code sign, but I still thought I might be able to lock the door before Dr. George was in view. I hurried out of the bathroom and into the hallway with the key in my hand.

But it was too late.

Dr. George was just fifteen feet away and approaching fast. Vince was on his tail like a little puppy dog. He bounced excitedly and was clearly trying desperately to distract the vice principal.

"Hey, Dr. George, hey!" Vince chattered as he bounced along behind him. "Are you sure you don't want to hear more about my pet turtle, Billiam? Because I swear he's the greatest turtle ever, really! One time I made him a castle, and you should have seen the way he lorded over the peasant frogs I stuck inside of it with him. He was a natural, if I don't say so myself!

"Oh, and this one time I also made him a little Hula-Hoop out of these magic rings I stole from a Canadian magician. I even took the turtle out of his shell so he could use the Hula-Hoop. Except, man, he really didn't want to come out. I finally was able to get him out with a big rock, but holy Yeltsin, did it ever make an awful mess of his shell house. Anyways, I think the ring still had magic on it because when I put it around the turtle he stopped moving and went into a coma; it was pretty sad. I still have the little guy. He's safe in his coma in my sock drawer, but one day I'm gonna find the counter spell to the Canadian's magic. Do you think it'd take a spell from a Mexican magician? Well, do ya?"

I had to keep back a laugh, because sadly enough that was a true story. But Vince was only in kindergarten at the time, so we hadn't known any better. I swear, too, once we found out that the turtle was dead and not in a coma, we both cried for like a week straight. We'd just wanted him to Hula-Hoop.

Dr. George was just a few feet away now, but Vince actually got him to stop and face him, buying me just enough time to pocket the bathroom key without being noticed.

"What is wrong with you?" Dr. George asked Vince in a way that I thought adults were never supposed to talk to children.

Vince just grinned at him.

"That is not an appropriate story to be telling, okay? Now get back to class before I give you detention!"

"But there's still recess for another three minutes,"

Vince said, keeping that dumb grin spread all over his face like butter on toast.

"Go!" Dr. George yelled.

Vince glanced at me, shrugged, and wandered off down the hall.

I made a move as if I was also just leaving, but Dr. George grabbed my shoulder with his crusty old hand. He grabbed it harder than any adult should ever grab a kid, and my knees almost buckled at the pain of his fingers digging into my arm.

"Get in there," he said, motioning toward the bathroom with his other hand.

"But I just finished. Why would I—"

"*Now*, Mr. Barrett," he hissed.

I let him guide me back inside the bathroom. He stopped in the middle and looked around as if he'd never been inside a bathroom before. I was afraid he was going to ask me for instructions or something.

"What's going on in here?" he asked.

"Uh, probably some kids using the bathroom," I said, rubbing my sore shoulder.

He raised his hand, and for a moment I thought he was going to slap me, so I flinched. Then he laughed and merely rubbed his stiff fake hair and sighed. He coughed and then jabbed his finger in my chest. Hard. His old bony pointer finger slammed into my sternum with enough force that I thought I heard my chest crack in half.

"You are a liar! I know you're up to something," he said, jabbing me with his finger once for every other word.

"I don't know what to say, sir," I said, trying to hold back the urge to poke him back right in his bulging eyeballs like in this old Three Stooges movie I saw once.

"Start by telling me what you were doing all the way down here. This bathroom is nowhere near your classrooms or the playgrounds."

I shrugged and looked at my feet.

"Well?" he asked.

I started crying. Not for real. It was just a ruse, of course. Being able to cry on demand is a pretty powerful tool when dealing with adults. But my aching shoulder and chest certainly didn't hurt my ability to cry right there on the spot.

"I'm too embarrassed to go in the other ones." I sobbed. "I get . . . *shy* in bathrooms where a lot of people go, okay?"

I could feel Dr. George's old, wrinkle-shaded eyes staring at the top of my head. He said nothing for the longest time. Finally I peeked up at him.

He was smiling. I'd never seen him smile before.

On his face a smirk looked about as natural as a blind, three-legged giraffe on stilts and roller skates would look trying to play centerfield in a major league baseball game.

"You think I'm going to buy that?" he asked.

I shrugged.

"Well, I don't, so cut the crap," he said, once again jabbing his finger at me to emphasize his words, only this time it stopped just short of my face. This guy sure loved to use his finger to make points. I wondered if he'd even be able to communicate with other human beings without it.

I didn't know what else to say, so I just looked him right in the eyes. It felt like I was looking into an emotional desert, a place where there is nothing but dry, hot, mean sand. He squinted and shoved past me.

He pushed back the swinging door to the trash can where all of my money and records were stashed and looked inside. He leaned down and moved his head from side to side, so he could see in at all angles. Then he reached down in and pulled out a mashed ball of paper towels.

Dr. George scowled and stuffed them back inside. He wiped his hand on his suit pants. I tried not to breathe my sigh of relief too loudly. I'd stashed some damp paper towels on top of my stuff for extra cover, but what if he'd reached into the trash can just a little bit deeper?

Then he moved to the first stall and pushed the door open. When he saw that it was empty, Dr. George moved to the second stall and then on to the third, the very stall in which Joe sat on a toilet with my small desk and chairs resting on his lap. He was probably dying from the weight and panic. The door didn't budge when Dr. George pushed.

"Occupied," Joe's voice rang out.

"Who are you? I demand to know what's going on!" Dr. George said.

"Uh, do you *really* want to know what's going on in here?" Joe said.

"Stop this foolishness! I know trouble when I see it. Now what are you two up to?"

"Dude, there's only one of me in here, and I'm telling you, you don't want to know what's happening in here," Joe said. The desk must have been getting heavy because Joe's last few words strained as if he was being choked. Under the circumstances it actually sounded authentically gross, if you know what I mean.

Dr. George must have heard it, too, because his scowl disappeared and he looked uncertain for the first time.

"I still want—" He was cut off by the recess bell.

"Sir, that's the bell. It means I have to go back to class. Can I please go?" I begged while dancing impatiently.

"I know what that bell was." Dr. George sneered as he glanced at his watch and then walked toward the bathroom door. "I have an important meeting right now, but I'm going to find out what sort of racket you've got going on in here, Mr. Barrett. You'd better believe that. How does one more day of detention sound in the meantime?"

"For what?"

"Okay, you want two?"

I kept my mouth shut, figuring that there was no response I could give that wouldn't result in more detention.

With that he nodded and showed me his teeth in what I can only imagine was another attempt at a smile. Then he was gone. I waited a few moments to make sure he wasn't coming back and then I quickly helped Joe put the desk back. Fred came back, and I hooked up the DVRs again and then locked the bathroom from the outside.

"What are we going to do, Mac?" Joe asked.

"I don't know," I said, "but you guys better get to class. We can't all be in detention today. We still have a business to run."

Chapter 14

Monday—Lower Grade Playground

At lunch that day we decided to just close up the office. Joe hung the "Closed for Repairs" sign on the door so kids knew that we'd be out indefinitely. We needed to lay low right now, at least until we could figure how to get Dr. George off our tails.

I let Fred do whatever he wanted for the rest of the day and sent Joe on a few errands for some of the customers I'd seen the past few days. Vince and I went outside to the playground to brainstorm.

"Before we get down to business, I need to ask you something," I said.

"Okay, shoot."

"What's the Cubs' longest winning streak in team history?"

"You realize that I'm not a moron, right?" he asked.

I shrugged. "Could have fooled me, Joe Blanton lover."

Vince scoffed theatrically and then kicked some pebbles down the hill. We were headed to the new playground by the Shed for privacy reasons. We couldn't be too careful.

"Twenty-one games. They did it twice, once in 1880 and again in 1935. Both currently stand as tied for the second-longest winning streaks in baseball history."

"Wow, that was so much more information than I asked for. Thanks for wasting ten seconds of my life, Mr. Show-off," I said.

Vince laughed as we reached the playground and sat on the swings, but his laughter sounded pretty vacant. I was pretty sure he was thinking the same thing I was.

"So," I said, "are we ever going to get to use the office again? I mean, now that we know George is onto us, it may not be safe to open up shop in there."

Vince shook his head. The look on his face seemed about as bleak as the gravel under our feet, which was destined to sit there forever getting trampled by kids.

"What are we going to do, Vince? Without the office we pretty much don't have a business."

"I know, I know. We'll figure something out," he said. "Or I mean, you will, right?"

"Hey, hey, I'm not Joe Blanton. I can't work miracles,"

I said. "But maybe even more important is figuring out more about the SMARTs. I hope Tyrell comes through for us, because if our school doesn't pass those, then there'll definitely be no business for us."

Vince nodded solemnly, and I started getting too bummed so I decided to change the subject.

"Did I tell you yet that I got to dance with Hannah?"

Vince's jaw dropped. Then he composed himself. "Whatever. I'm not that stupid."

"No, seriously, Vince. In gym class we did dancing, and I got paired up with her. She was actually really nice."

Vince shook his head and kicked at the sandy gravel under his feet. It made me nervous that he wasn't saying anything. Then he sighed.

"Well, she's a liar. Remember that, Mac? So don't get fooled. She was probably just, like, selling her lies, you know?" Vince said.

My first impulse was to call *him* a liar and then kick sand in his face, but the more I thought about it the more I realized he was probably right. She was blinding me, making me into an idiot by being nice to me. And I'd fallen for it like a chump.

"Yeah, you're probably right. It was still weird, though. But at least I now know for sure that something really strange is going on around here. I mean, the fried school lunches, the weird gym classes, someone dumping poop into kids' lockers, kids not getting punished for fighting, and on and on. I mean, for all of this stuff to be happening at the same time . . . well, it all had to be related somehow. Didn't it? I mean, all of this stuff adding together is so bad that they even brought in Dr. George to try and fix it."

Vince nodded slowly. "Yeah, it all must be related. But why? Why would anyone do this, and who would have the power to do all of that stuff?"

"Definitely a school employee," I said.

"Oh man, Mac!" Vince said. "I can't believe I never connected the dots before."

"What?"

"What other major event occurred right around the time these weird things started happening? Right before George showed up to fix everything?"

It hit me. Mr. Kjelson. Mr. Kjelson started here just a few months ago.

"Coach Kjelson," I said, not wanting to make that connection. "Maybe Hannah actually has been right all along. That still doesn't explain why she lied about dating Mr. Kjelson's son, but still . . ."

"Exactly," Vince said, shaking his head slowly with

a look of pain on his face. It was always a tragic thing to discover a fellow Cubs fan might be up to no good. Especially a guy as cool as Kjelson had seemed to be. "I mean, that can't just be a coincidence, can it?"

"I don't think we can afford to assume it is," I agreed. "So now we need to figure out if Kjelson is somehow behind this all. And why would he want to take down the school? All this in addition to finding a way to take down George before he shuts down our business and trying to figure out how to make sure we all pass the SMARTs. Great."

Vince didn't have much to add so he just kept shaking his head, still mourning the possible corruption of a Cubs fan.

"Right. What should we do about George?" Vince asked.

"We need some dirt on the guy. Maybe Tyrell can dig up something on him, or we could do some espionage work ourselves and see what we can find in his office or something," I said.

"Isn't that going to be dangerous?"

"What choice do we have? We have to do *something*."

"Good point," Vince conceded.

"Anyways, you help out Joe after school with some of the other customers. At detention I'm going to confront Hannah and see why she lied to us. There's something more to all of this, and I have a bad feeling about it."

Vince nodded and looked at his feet. "Oh, okay. Yeah, that's cool."

"What's the matter with you?"

"I don't know. I just thought we could maybe do a dual interview. I kind of like that girl for some reason," he said. "Besides, she already fooled you into a false sense of security once today."

I laughed and said, "Hey, stay focused, Vince. We have other customers, you know? Customers who have actually paid us. We need to focus on them. Plus, don't worry about me; I'm onto her tricks now."

Even as we walked back toward the school, I kept wondering why I was so worried about Hannah. Really, I should have been handling the other problems for paying customers. And why *couldn't* Vince come with me to talk to Hannah? He'd always handled her better than me anyways. I didn't know why, but I couldn't really come up with any answers to those questions, and that bothered me most of all.

In class that afternoon Mr. Skari announced that the whole school would be taking the SMARTs the next day. Which gave me basically no time to figure out how the tests worked and whether I needed to intervene and also how I would even be able to do that. Most everyone in the class groaned after the announcement and I did, too, but for slightly different reasons.

There was still a chance that Tyrell could come through with some info for me. After all, the day didn't end when school did, but it was a long shot. I mean, Tyrell was good, sure, but was he that good? Could anyone be that good?

And thing was, the way Mr. Skari acted next convinced me more than ever that I needed to do something. Ever since last Wednesday we'd been doing nothing but SMART-based worksheet packets and taking practice tests. And now he was up front announcing to all of us that we'd done all right on them—but that that wasn't enough.

"This last round of practice tests went okay but barely. It would be much better if we had another week to hone your skills." There was a glimmer of desperation that I'd never seen in him before.

Mr. Skari was a big dude, bigger than my dad, maybe the tallest guy I'd ever seen in person. But he also was pretty calm, laid back about most things, except for staying on schedule, of course. Which is part of why I liked him as a teacher: he wasn't tightly wound like a lot of the other teachers. Except for now, when dealing with these SMARTs, he was acting like he was more tightly wound than a fishing reel with a twenty-foot, three-ton shark on the other end.

So he really pushed us hard the rest of the day, which stunk because Mondays are bad enough as is. But if anything, all he did was make the already panicked kids so panicked that I thought for sure a riot was going to break out or at the very least some heads would explode.

I decided to stick around after class to ask about the SMARTs. See what he might be able to tell me. I had detention from the incident with George that morning in the fourth stall, but since Mr. Skari was a teacher, he could write me a late excuse note.

"What can I help you with, Baretta?"

I have no idea why Mr. Skari sometimes called me that; he was always making up weird nicknames for kids. Some kids thought it just made him weird, but most of us liked it. Anything abnormal that teachers did usually was a good thing. It kept school more interesting, because otherwise it got old and boring after, like, the second day of school every year. Mr. Skari already stood out because it wasn't every day you came across a six-foot-six-inch-tall elementary school teacher.

"Why are these tests so important?" I asked. "I mean, even you teachers seem pretty worried."

"Well, it's because they're a reflection of how well the school is doing. To all of the most important people.

The people who make decisions about the school and its staff."

I nodded, but I wasn't sure I understood completely. He made it seem like this test was all that mattered, like all of the other stuff we did all year long was just for show and counted for nothing.

"I heard that this test could get the school closed down. Is that true?"

"Oh." Mr. Skari smiled hollowly. "Well, don't worry about that kind of stuff. Just do the best you can."

I let it go, but his answer worried me. Or I guess I should say his lack of an answer worried me. He maybe thought I was too young to notice that he'd dodged the question, that he didn't really deny it, but I practically invented question dodging so I didn't miss it. Basically he had just told me the answer was yes without really saying anything at all.

"Who grades the tests? Like, how do they work? I mean, if they're so important, then shouldn't our teachers be grading them?"

At this Mr. Skari actually laughed. "I think I have some stuff to do, and if I'm not mistaken, I have it down here that you're actually supposed to be in detention right now."

I also wasn't too young to know what this was: an end to the conversation.

I nodded, and he handed me my late pass. I left not really feeling better at all, even though I'd found out plenty. In fact I felt worse because I now knew that these tests were just as important to the Suits in charge of this place as we'd all feared. And our window to do something about them was closing fast.

Chapter 15

Monday—The Detention Room

I was surprised to see that Hannah was not in detention. I sat by myself in the corner and tried to keep from staring at the door the whole time. I kept expecting her suddenly to show up looking too calm to be late for detention. I was actually pretty excited about confronting her. I wanted to see how she would talk her way out of this one—the fact that I knew Kjelson didn't even have a son.

But she never showed up.

Luckily, though, I had a pretty good idea where I might find her.

Outside of attending school assemblies and plays for fun, I'd only been in the Olson Olson Theatre a few times before. Once was for an eighth-grade orchestra recital that I'd needed to attend for business purposes, and the other time was when I was in a play myself in the fourth grade. And after that experience I vowed to never be in another play again, even though our school was actually pretty famous locally for having the best school plays in the state.

The play had been called *Medicare and You*. A local theater company had been in charge and not the school's usual drama teacher. They wanted us to perform it for some senior citizens they bused in from a local retirement home, and they used some of our fourth and fifth graders in it, since old people like to watch little kids perform plays, I guess. I played this character called Donald Deductible. I had no idea what anything I said in that play meant. It was probably the most confusing play in the history of the world. I'm pretty sure I played a good guy because I had to keep hugging Billy, who played a retired person. They had him all decked out in creepy wrinkle makeup; it was horrifying. He looked like some kind of midget witch with a bad case of acne. But I don't think any of the other characters seemed like good guys, especially this one called Coverage Guidelines Gus. He was the worst, I thought. Anyways, I don't think the old people liked the play too much either, because by the end half of them were snoring and one old lady started screaming something about being stuck inside of a donut hole.

The Olson Olson Theatre still pretty much looked the same now as it had then. As you entered you were at the top of one of two sets of stairs, with rows of nice leather seats on either side that ran down to the large stage. Behind the middle section of seats way in the back was the production booth, where the sound and lighting people worked. Up above that was a small balcony that was used for seating when the place got really packed.

It was a really nice and expensive theater. The money for it had been donated to the school by two guys named Olson. But they weren't even related. One of the Olsons was simply a big theater fan, and he'd heard about our school and how great our plays were, and he's a really rich dude, and so when he came and liked our plays, he decided to help build us a new theater. Because before that the school theater was about as old and rickety as a hundred-and-five-year-old man. Comparing the new theater to the old theater would be like comparing an ancient Nintendo 64 with the newest version of the Xbox: there was simply no comparison.

Anyway, then there was this other guy, the other Olson, and he was a former student. Our drama teacher has been at the school forever, and he was why our school plays were so good. So this guy Olson was in theater a long time ago, and he'd said it changed his life. And now that he's a rich and famous actor, he wanted to give back to our school. The thing was that both Olsons wanted to donate the new theater. It was actually a pretty funny fiasco for a while, with those two guys fighting in the local papers all the time. The thing was, each of them wanted the theater to be named after him, which I heard my dad say once was pretty typical for actors and rich people. "Always in need of more attention" is what he'd said.

So the two Olsons fought over whose name would get to be on the new theater. Then finally someone was just like, "Hey, you have the same name. Why not just call it Olson Theatre?" But neither Olson liked that idea either because then you'd never know which Olson it was. So eventually after like three months of arguing, the two Olsons agreed to split the costs and name the theater after both of them.

And so they built us this awesome new theater and its full name is: The Monte Andrew Garrison Geoffrey Olson Olson Theatre. Most kids just call it the Magoo Theatre, which I think is probably the most fitting name anyway.

I entered the theater on the left side and stood by the wall. The school's play director and drama teacher,

Dewey Louie-Booey (no, that's not a joke), stood in front of the stage giving out directions to six giant sunflowers with arms and legs while a couple of kids dressed in all-black spandex suits and fake, ten-inch fingernails stood to the side watching. The yellow-foam flower petals the sunflower kids wore around their faces were so heavy that one kid tipped over.

What was so great about Louie-Booey's plays was that he wrote them all himself. Every play our school did was a Louie-Booey original instead of some cheap and crappy version of *Annie* or whatever other junky plays other schools were doing these days. And one of the best things about Louie-Booey, and what made him particularly awesome, was that he let the kids get involved, really involved. Like, he let them all interpret their own parts and help design their own costumes. So the school plays really felt like something that our students *created* as opposed to just a bunch of kids following directions from an adult.

Everyone loved Louie-Booey and his plays, anyway, and the fact that he then let kids put their own spin on their character and really own the play in a cool way took it over the top. So at our school almost everybody wanted to be in plays, not just the drama kids who liked to both sing and complain a lot. At our school even the athletes liked to be in the plays. There was sometimes a waiting list to get to be in the next play, even if the part was just as an extra.

Just as an example of how awesome our school plays were: our last one started out with a scene where Kanye West and a lobster were walking through a desert, and then they got into this awesome shoot-out with these mutant cacti. Anyway, you probably needed to see it to understand how great it was.

"Okay!" Louie-Booey yelled, but not in a mean way, just loud. "You need to really get into your characters. You are flowers grown in the earth. Your seeds will eventually be harvested and become crunchy, salty snacks at sporting events everywhere. How does that make you feel?"

The kids on stage giggled. Louie-Booey had this sense of humor where he would say ridiculous things all seriouslike, but then there'd be this grin on his face. Anyway, it's hard to describe, but the guy was pretty funny.

The sunflowers started talking to each other, and then they started acting like sunflowers, assuming sunflowers really could walk and talk. And I have to say, they looked pretty good—and funny. That was the other thing about our school plays: most of them were meant to be funny; they were comedies. Which everybody loved because really, who wants to see a play about an orphaned homeless girl or about a war where people die? I mean, those plays are just depressing. Plus, it's fun to see kids get to try and be funny on purpose on stage.

Louie-Booey laughed at the sunflowers. The sight on stage would have been the most disturbing thing I'd seen since this one time when I saw Vince's grandma eating from a tub of Vaseline with a spoon if it wasn't also so funny.

"Yes, yes, now's the time for the Underlings of St. Crispin to come in and plague the sunflowers. *Now*, Underlings!" Louie-Booey yelled through his laughter.

The kids in black spandex, who apparently were Underlings of St. Crispin, started shuffling toward the sunflowers. Except they didn't walk normally; they spread their legs really far apart and took high, huge exaggerated steps as if they were in a minefield. They wiggled their long fingernails in front of them as they neared.

"Okay, now it's time for the Articles of Vespa!" Louie-Booey yelled. "Where are you, Articles?"

The Articles of Vespa entered the stage from behind the curtain. There were four of them, each wearing a different costume. The first one was dressed up as a giant pair of scissors. At first I thought the next two were supposed to be those cartoon characters Rocky and

Bullwinkle, but I wasn't sure, because the kid dressed as the squirrel had foam all over his mouth, so I think he was simply supposed to be a rabid squirrel. Plus, the moose was wearing a Hawaiian shirt and a grass skirt. The last Article of Vespa was a giant tube of toothpaste, except that the brand name crudely drawn on the costume said "Cavity Growers Tooth-pasties."

Then the Articles of Vespa started chanting.

"We want to drop the eggs! But the Formica is too cold. We want to drop the eggs! But the Formica is too cold."

I held in a laugh. It was pretty clear our next play might be the funniest one yet. Maybe the weirdest, too, but that was probably why it would also be the funniest. I decided to move along so I didn't ruin it for myself once the show opened. I know going to plays is usually kind of nerdy at a lot of schools, but at our school everybody went to the plays. Every showing sold out.

I moved around to the other side of the theater and knocked on the door to the production booth as gently as I could. After a few seconds the door opened a crack. I saw nothing in that open sliver but darkness, and then suddenly a face appeared in front of me.

It was some kid I recognized as a seventh grader, but he didn't look much older than me. He had thin metal glasses and short blond hair. His eyes bulged from his head like a pug dog's.

"Do you have the filter?" he asked.

"Um, no."

His face disappeared into the darkness, and I heard whispering. Then he was back.

"Why not?" he said.

"What?"

"Where's the filter? We need it."

A small bead of sweat trickled down his face and across his nose.

"I'm sorry. I don't have it. I just need to speak with Hannah," I said.

His face disappeared again, and I heard more whispering. *"No, he said he doesn't have it. I don't know. Maybe he's hiding it."*

Then he was back.

"Hannah is not here," he said.

"If you get her for me, I'll get you the filter," I said.

His eyes bulged even more, and for a second I thought they'd splatter all over the inside of his glasses like bugs hitting a windshield.

"Hold on," he said.

I waited while he disappeared back into the small production room. After a few minutes I was ready to give up and leave, but then Hannah came out of the booth and closed the door behind her.

"What are you doing here?" she whispered.

"I need to talk to you," I said.

She looked at me. Her green eyes glowed even in the dark light of the theater. I waited, she continued to look at me, and then she shuffled her feet and frowned.

"Well, start talking," she hissed.

"Tell me about Bryce," I said.

"What? I already did. What's wrong with you?" she asked.

"I don't like being lied to."

She grabbed my shirt and pulled me out of the theater and into the hallway.

"What are you talking about? I'm busy, okay? Just tell me what you want."

"Mr. Kjelson doesn't have a son, *okay*? I found out. So you want to tell me why you really came to me for help?"

She looked neither surprised nor upset at my revelation. Actually, she looked calmer than I'd ever seen her. Almost like I was really seeing her dropping her act for the first time. She sighed.

"It's complicated, okay? I just thought it'd be easier to make up that stupid story," she said.

"Fair enough. Now what's the real reason?"

"You wouldn't understand."

"I bet I would," I said.

That's when she giggled and shook her head. I

watched uncomfortably as she laughed.

"What? What's so funny?"

"Sorry," she said. "I was just picturing you trying to understand anything at all."

I shook my head. We'd gotten along so well earlier that morning. But I guess that had been part of the lie. "Look, you haven't paid me yet, so maybe it's just best if we cancel this. I can't really do much for clients who keep lying to me."

She frowned and nodded. I started walking away, a little upset with myself for doing that. I *never* gave up on problems. Ever. But in this case I couldn't really even tell anymore what it was that I needed to do.

"Wait, Mac," she called out. "Did you ask him about me?"

I turned around as she walked up to me. I nodded.

"And?" she said.

"And, yeah, okay. I admit he kinda, sorta acted pretty weird."

She looked at me again like she had before, like she was finally being honest. "Please do this for me?" She shook her head as if she was completely dismissing all of the lies she'd told me. "There's nowhere I can turn. I already tried going to the principals, even. He followed me here. I used to go to Oaks Crossing, and even there he had it in for me. It all started when I made a joke about how short he is. I kinda sorta got a whole bunch of kids to start calling him a midget. I know, totally childish, believe me. But anyway, he got his revenge by giving me detention, way more than I deserved. He, like, basically made it his mission to make my life there a living nightmare.

"So that's why I transferred here this year. To get away from him. You think I wanted to leave all my friends back at Oaks Crossing to come here? Well, I didn't at all. But he followed me. I know he transferred here to get me. I'm sure of it. I seriously just made up that thing about Bryce because it was so much simpler and more believable than the truth. I mean, it sounds ridiculous even now, me explaining it to you. I need your help, Mac. You're the last hope I have to get away from him."

I could see that she was close to tears now. And even I had to admit that things must've been pretty bad if she transferred schools to get away from this guy. She had even gone to Dickerson and George for help. I'd never have done that no matter how bad things got.

Then Hannah removed a twenty-dollar bill from her pocket and held it out to me. It fluttered between her index and middle fingers.

"I'll pay you now. Full asking price. Then you'll take care of Kjelson? You'll just get him out of here so he can't keep making my life miserable?"

I hesitated. But my business ethics got the better of me. I took the money. Never turn down a customer when they're offering cash up front. And never give up on a customer. Plus, if she was telling the truth, then Kjelson had to be stopped. Nobody deserved that kind of teacher. Also, there was Vince's new theory that perhaps Kjelson was somehow a part of all the school's other problems as well, considering that they started up shortly after he started teaching here. I had to admit that there was at least a chance that Hannah was right about him.

"Okay, deal. I'll get him off your back. No more questions. No more lies, though, okay?"

She nodded and smiled. Once again, like this morning in gym, she looked like a normal girl and not someone who'd just as soon grind you up to make fertilizer as she would be nice to you.

"Thanks, Mac," she said sweetly.

Chapter 16

Monday—Bedroom

Before heading home that day after school, I stopped by Vince's trailer for a while. I told him about my exchange with Hannah, and after that he was even more convinced that Kjelson was up to no good. But he was also more confused than ever. Why would a new teacher be so obsessed with getting a school in trouble with the higher-up Suits? I wished I had an answer for him, but I was probably even more confused than he was so we left it at that.

When I got home, I went straight up to my room. I had just about an hour before dinner would be ready, and I wanted to make some notes in my Books, which I had brought home for the night, before I ate. It's always best to take care of any business you have before eating. Because after eating one of my mom's dinners, all you'll want to do is lie on the couch while a cheesy game show plays on the TV and wonder why you ate so much.

I flipped on the lights, closed the door, and turned to face my desk. And then I almost let out an embarrassing yell that would have shattered all the windows in the house.

"Hi, Mac."

Tyrell was sitting in the chair by my desk.

"You have to stop doing that to me," I said. "Do my parents even know you're here?"

He looked a little taken aback. "No, why would they?"

You just had to love this kid. He didn't understand the concept of lawful entry. To him the only way to enter or exit a location was undetected, and I didn't think using a front door or a doorbell was a thought that ever crossed his mind.

"So you've been just sitting here in the dark waiting for me to get home like some kind of serial killer or something?"

Tyrell grinned. "No, of course not. I knew right about what time you'd get here. So no worries, I haven't been waiting long."

I chuckled. "I hope this means you have good news for me?"

"That depends. I have a lot of information for you, but it will be up to you to decide whether it's good or bad."

"Is it about the SMARTs?"

Tyrell nodded.

"Well, let me get Vince and Joe over here, then, because if we're going to plan something, we'll have to do it tonight since the school is taking the test tomorrow."

I called Joe and Vince and invited them over for dinner. My mom had an open-table policy for dinner. Which meant I never even had to get her permission. I could basically just invite over whoever I wanted for dinner. Which, of course, was awesome.

After dinner I told my mom we were headed to the school to play football. And, well, we were headed to the school, just not to play football. Tyrell, Joe, Vince, and I all went to my office in the fourth stall to discuss the SMARTs.

Meeting there during school hours had been dangerous because of George's recent suspicion, but it was now seven thirty at night, so we figured there was no chance anybody would be around. Which is why it was the perfect—no, *the only* safe place to meet to discuss a possible plan that involved cheating on a state administered test—something that I didn't think had ever been attempted on such a large scale before in history.

"Okay, Tyrell," I said once we were all grouped inside my office. "What do you have for us?"

Now, I'd like to say that what he found out was pretty good, considering he had only half a day to do it, but that would be a lie. The truth was he'd found out so much information that it was close to a miracle. It wasn't just pretty good; it was better than was humanly possible. Tyrell would put CIA agents to shame. He could out-cool and out-spy James Bond with nothing but a used toothbrush and seventeen cents.

Tyrell had discovered that the SMARTs were administered via those sheets that just had circles all over them. The kind where you fill in A, B, C, D, or E with a pencil for hundreds of questions. The questions came in a separate packet. After the test Dr. George and his secretaries would go around to each classroom and collect all of the answer sheets for the entire school. Then they would go back to his office and put them all together in one large security envelope and seal it. At six thirty the next morning a few guys from the State Testing Bureau, or STB, would arrive and take the test results back to their local facility. The answer sheets were fed into a large machine, and because of some new software they got recently, the scores could be generated and delivered back to the school within a day or two.

Also, one last thing Tyrell discovered was that each

school that gave the test got one master copy of the test booklet that contained all of the correct test answers for all grades. Tyrell said our school's copy of the master booklet had been hand delivered to Dr. George (Tyrell witnessed this exchange happen), and since that time, it has been sitting in Dr. George's office in a locked drawer in his desk, third down on the right side.

I shook my head and looked at Vince after Tyrell had finished. The kid was amazing.

"How did you possibly find out all of this?" I asked.

Tyrell smiled. "Mac, you know I can't tell you that."

I nodded. Tyrell was more open with me than anyone, but he was still pretty secretive about his methods. He always said it was more for our own protection than for his that he did not tell us, but either way he was probably right: I almost didn't even want to know.

"Well, the problem is that sounds pretty airtight," I said. "The answers go from the classroom right to Dr. George right to a sealed security envelope. And even if we did get the master booklet somehow, there's likely not enough time anymore to get a copy of it to every kid in the school. Plus, then we'd have to deal with possible narks, and that's not even mentioning how bush league that would be. I mean, if one kid gets caught with a copy of the master booklet, then the whole operation would backfire worse than when the

Yankees gave Jeter a huge contract extension when he was already well past his prime."

Joe and Vince agreed. Despite all of Tyrell's great work it still seemed like there wouldn't be much we could do at this point.

"Well, maybe that's okay," Vince said. "I mean, do you really think everyone is going to fail?"

I shrugged. "Maybe, maybe not. But more than that, think about the money behind this, Vince." I reached into my backpack and took out my Books, flipped through them, and did a quick tally. "I mean, if you add up all the offers we've gotten from kids who want help cheating on the SMARTs, then we'll make over one thousand dollars! That's more than we've ever made from one single operation, by a ton. Can you imagine?"

Vince nodded. He knew it, too—that was a lot of bread. Plus, then we'd also have peace of mind knowing that our school would pass with flying colors, teachers and students would be happy, and so on.

"Okay, sure, but that still doesn't help us figure out how we'll pull this off," Vince said.

"What about, like, intercepting the test scores on their way to the testing facility?" Joe said. "We'll just need to take out the STB guys and grab the tests from them."

I assumed he was joking, so I laughed. "Right, well, I haven't quite moved up to armed robbery just yet, Joe."

"If only Joe Blanton was here," Vince said. "He'd know what to do."

"Yeah, he'd probably just bribe the STB office," I said. "And then he'd let them score eight runs in one inning of bribery."

Vince scoffed. "That one doesn't even make sense, Mac."

"Guys!" Joe said. "Focus."

He was right; we needed to figure this out.

"Well," I began, "this would be no small job . . . but we could break into the administration offices at five o'clock, after practice, and after everyone else has gone home, and change all of the answers ourselves."

Everyone stared at me for a moment. They could tell I was serious, and maybe that's what scared them most.

Vince was the first to speak. "Mac, if you're even suggesting this, I'm assuming you know how much of a risk this is, so I won't even go into that. But even then, how do we get the answer sheets out of the security envelope without it being obvious that they were tampered with?"

Then Tyrell, who had been pretty quiet since sharing all of his research with us, said, "Oh, that's not a problem. While doing my investigation, I was able to lift a couple SMART security envelopes off of one of the STB administrators I'd been tailing."

He pulled out a few large, sturdy yellow envelopes from his bag.

"Nice," Joe said. Vince nodded.

"We'll just need to switch the school bar code and stuff off of the real envelopes to these when we're all done. Which I think I can do pretty easily with an X-acto knife and some Gorilla glue."

"That just leaves the question of how we'll break in to get both the answer sheets and the master booklet," I said.

Tyrell grinned. "Guys, I've got you covered there, too."

Chapter 17

Tuesday—Mr. Skari's Classroom

The SMART testing started pretty much right away Tuesday morning. Apparently the tests were so long and hard that they lasted all day. Mr. Skari started out with a lecture about the importance of using a number two pencil—seriously, I half expected them to wheel in a rickety, rusty guillotine for those of us who dared use a pen or mythical number three lead pencil. Then we began the first part of the test.

I wasn't too nervous, really, even after all I'd heard about how hard it was, *and* even after Skari went on and on about how failing this test could result in being held back a year. Because I'm usually pretty good at tests. After dealing with the sort of crap I do each day, who wouldn't be good at a simple school test?

But the SMART was not just another simple test. It was actually a lot harder than I expected it to be.

No fewer than four kids in my class broke down crying right in the middle of it, and the sound of snapping pencils clicked throughout the room like a miniature Fourth of July celebration. The test was definitely hard. Which drove out any last-second thoughts about ditching our plan, because if we wanted to make sure the school passed, the plan would need to be put into effect.

The first part of the test ended just before morning recess. Joe, Vince, and Fred met up with me outside the East Wing boys' bathroom. We didn't open up the office that day because we were still wary of George lurking in the area. But I did hand each of them a list of kids.

"These are the kids who paid for help with the SMART. Let's use recesses and lunch periods today to track down the kids on your list and let them know not to worry about the test too much, that we've got it all taken care of."

The truth was I was going to doctor everybody's answers, not just the kids who had paid me. That way we could be sure the school would pass. But I still needed to tell only a few kids. I mean, once a few kids know something, everyone will know within an hour usually. That's how schools work.

The rest of the test that day was about the same, but as the day went on, kids seemed less and less stressed. It was pretty clear that word was getting around. In fact, during afternoon recess the last few kids on my list already knew about what I was going to do by the time I went to go see them. And in the halls I got a lot of kids patting me on the back and thanking me, and one cute seventh-grade girl even wanted to give me a hug, which was kind of embarrassing but I let her anyway.

After school Vince and I went to baseball tryouts. Once again I'm pretty sure Vince made quite the impression. I noticed that Kjelson spent a lot of time watching kids chase after Vince's filthy breaking pitches. The best part about Vince's arm was that his pitches were so clean. A lot of his movement was generated by his grip, so his throwing motion stayed really sound; there was hardly any extra strain on his elbow. And that also meant that it was going to be near impossible for batters to get tipped off by his delivery because it was identical every time, no matter what he was throwing.

I know Vince is only a sixth grader, but in my opinion it wasn't too early to already be thinking about the majors. I mean, he could definitely already strike out Joe Blanton, even as a sixth grader, so I couldn't even imagine how good he'd be by the time he graduated high school.

Practice ended a little early that day because Kjelson said he had some "important matters to attend to," which was actually great. We were going to need all the time we could get to execute our plan before the janitors made their final sweep of the school at six. I've said that the janitor and I had an understanding, and that was true, but he'd always been pretty clear to me that he still had to do his job, part of which was making sure that all kids were out of the building when he locked up and left at six.

Vince and I changed as quickly as we could and then headed down toward the south side of the school, where the administration offices were located. It was 4:15 already, so chances were that the secretaries and principals would either be gone or leaving soon. They were almost always gone by four thirty.

Vince and I walked by the admin offices and saw that one secretary and Dr. George were still there so we just kept on walking by. We veered into the school library, which stayed open until four thirty.

We normally liked to avoid the library at all costs. Not because we hated books or anything, but because it was Snitch Town. If you needed a snitch or squealer, the library was the place to go. And you know how I feel about snitches, so it should be obvious why we avoided the library much the same way the entire student body avoided Chet, the kid with head lice.

But we were there because from the table nearest the door we could see the administration offices. We could keep watch without looking too suspicious. Normally kids hanging around the school hallways until four thirty wasn't a big deal, but normally we didn't have Dr. George after us. All we needed was to get caught loitering in the hallways and our whole operation would be ruined.

We sat across from each other at one of the small reading tables, sitting in silence for about fifteen minutes or so. Vince pretended to read a book, and I tried to ignore the sniveling stares of a few rats seated at the tables around us. I could feel their predatory eyes on me, waiting, desperate to tattle on me to the librarian for something or another.

As the minutes passed, more and more of them got up to leave. Then it was just Vince and I left. I'd seen the secretary leave, but Dr. George still hadn't walked out of the big wooden administration offices door. I guessed he was still getting all the SMART stuff ready to go for tomorrow morning, which is why he was still here later than usual.

Then finally, just as the clock hit 4:30 and the librarian started to kick us out, I saw Dr. George come striding out of his office. He flipped off the lights behind him and then headed for the south exit, away from the library.

"Bye, Mrs. Hunter," I said to the librarian as Vince and I pretended to head back toward the gym. After we were sure that Mrs. Hunter had also left the building, we circled back around to the administration offices.

I took out a digital walkie-talkie that Tyrell had given me the night before and switched it on.

"The Bacon has been fully smoked," I said into it, signaling Tyrell to head to the north school entrance.

Then Vince and I headed there ourselves. The doors all locked on the outside at four o'clock, so we had to go down and let Tyrell and our hired help inside. Changing the answers to several hundred tests in less than two hours would take more than just a few kids, so I'd hired some help.

Tyrell came inside, followed by Joe, Kitten, Fred, Great White, the Hutt, and several other bullies I'd hired in the past: Little Paul, Nubby, Kevin, and PrepSchool. Hiring bullies to help you with a delicate operation like this might seem like a stupid thing to do, but in actuality a lot of bullies are pros at cheating and breaking rules, so I thought they seemed like a natural choice. Plus, I know for certain that the last thing any of these bullies would do is squeal. If you want to stay on top at our school as a bully, then you can't be a squealer; it's that simple.

Plus, these bullies had helped a lot with a huge

problem I'd faced down just a few months ago, so I knew I could trust them . . . well, as much as you could really trust any bully, that is.

"Okay, Tyrell, after you," I said, pointing toward the door to the administration offices.

We moved down the hall and stopped in front of the big wooden door. Tyrell took off his backpack, dug inside it, and removed a small metal object.

"What is that?" Joe asked.

Tyrell didn't answer. He stood up just enough to reach the lock. The small metal object in his hand looked kind of like a gun. It had two thin, curved pieces of metal that squeezed together, like a curved pair of scissors. He then took out a small black pouch and removed a thin, flat metal rod about five inches long. He stuck it into the end of the gunlike object. Then he removed another small metal rod; this one was shaped like an L but with a few flat notches on the end. He stuck the ends of both rods into the door's lock. He squeezed the "trigger," and several loud clicking sounds echoed through the hallway. Tyrell didn't react to my sharp inhale, and he twisted the metal object sharply as he squeezed the trigger. It turned, and I heard the distinct click of the dead bolt sliding into the door.

He turned the handle and pushed the door open a few feet.

"Okay, okay, wait," Vince said. "What is that, and where the heck did you get it?"

Tyrell shrugged. "The internet."

He held the door open as we filed inside the administration office area. It was still barely light enough outside that we could see where we were going, since the whole back wall was lined with windows.

Fred stayed right near the door to keep watch as we'd all discussed earlier. Just in case a teacher came by or something, we would hopefully have enough warning to get out of sight.

We crouched to stay lower than the windows as we shuffled over to the door to Dr. George's office. We'd decided that for this part of the plan, Tyrell should go in alone. He knew where everything would be, and we didn't really think that having eleven kids, including several bullies, tromping through Dr. George's office was a particularly good idea, since it would be more likely that he'd notice someone had been in his office.

Tyrell worked his lock-pick magic on George's office and disappeared inside behind the door. It only took him a few minutes before he returned with the security envelopes full of answer sheets and the master booklet. I grinned at him, and he merely nodded back.

We carefully extracted the answer sheets from a cut Tyrell had made in the side of the envelopes while Joe made copies of the master booklet at a nearby copy machine. The copy machine seemed so loud in the quiet office that I half expected it to just explode and cover us all in ink and paper shreds while simultaneously setting off an alarm of some kind.

Then we passed out the copied master answer keys, and Joe dumped out a pile of erasers and number two pencils onto the floor. Tyrell and I put the stack of student answer sheets, which seemed like it was two stories high, on a side table sitting against the wall. I went over the instructions again: answer most of the questions right but leave a couple wrong. If the whole school scored one hundred percent, it would look suspicious.

Then we got started. At first it wasn't so bad. Go through the answer sheet, erase any wrong responses, and fill in the circles for correct answers. Simple. And as I went along, I was even more sure this arrangement was the right move. The kids seemed to have done a lot worse than I'd expected. It was definitely as hard as advertised.

But after like forty-five minutes and fifty or so tests each, our wrists were aching. I could barely feel my fingers anymore, and the pile of eraser shavings around us looked like some dude with really dry skin had just got done running a cheese grater all over himself. And all of our fingers were coated in black graphite from the pencils. The only one of us not whining after an hour was Kitten, who just sat there calmly erasing and filling in circles.

While we worked on the tests, Tyrell was carefully cutting off the school bar code and labels applied to the security envelope, and then after that he'd use the glue to apply everything onto the envelope we'd brought with us.

It felt like we were in there forever, erasing and filling circles. Erasing and filling. Erase. Fill. Erase. Fill. It was incredibly boring, and like I said, hand cramps were killing me. But by the time we finished the last answer sheet and stacked them back into one neat pile, it was only 5:40. We'd done pretty well; we still had twenty minutes to spare.

I paid all of the bullies their hard-earned ten dollars, and then they split. I also told Joe and Fred, who looked like he'd fallen asleep while he was supposed to have been looking out, that they could go home as well.

Vince and I helped Tyrell get all of the tests into the new envelopes, and then we sealed them up. Tyrell planted them and the original master booklet back inside Dr. George's office. Then we all left, making sure to pick up as many of the eraser shavings as we could. Tyrell disappeared like he always seems to, and then

Vince and I started down the hall toward the exit nearest our bike rack.

And then Kjelson came around the corner.

We stopped walking, and so did he. No one talked for a few moments—as if we'd both just caught each other in the act of doing something we weren't supposed to be doing.

"What are you two still doing here?" he asked finally. "Practice ended well over an hour ago."

Kids were typically allowed to remain inside the school until five thirty because of sports practices and play rehearsals and stuff like that, but since Mr. Kjelson was our coach and knew our practice had ended a while ago, it was a little unusual that we were still there.

"Nothing. We were just helping a friend with some project he's working on in one of the science labs," Vince said.

Vince always had been the better on-the-spot liar.

Mr. Kjelson nodded and said, "Okay, you were on your way out, though, right? The janitor will be locking up soon."

We nodded.

"Okay, see you both Thursday at tryouts, then," he said, and then continued down the hall toward the administration area.

It seemed like he had bought it.

"Well, that was close, but we did it, Vince!" I said as we exited the building.

Vince grinned at me. It had been one of the biggest single operations in school history. I'd just successfully cheated for the entire school on a state administered test. I'd probably just saved the school, based on how many answers we'd had to change, and also had made over a thousand dollars in the process. We were feeling pretty good, and that left just two major problems: finding a way to get George off of our case and figuring out who was messing with the school.

Chapter 18

Wednesday—The East Wing Hallway

The next morning I woke up still feeling pretty good. When I got to school, all of the kids seemed to be in good spirits, too. As I headed to my office before class to write a few things in my Books, several kids stopped me to thank me for what I'd done. Spirits were high, that was obvious.

But that all came crashing down on me when I got to my office and found a visitor waiting for me. We hadn't been open for a few days now because of the threat of Dr. George busting us, so it was pretty surprising to have a visitor that morning. Especially when that visitor was a school employee.

"Mac, we need to talk," the janitor said as I approached.

My first thought was panic. Someone had found out

about our operation yesterday. But then I decided that wasn't possible, that we'd cleaned up after ourselves too well.

"Is this about Vince and me getting caught in Kjelson's room last week? You didn't get in trouble for loaning me the key did—"

"It's not that, Mac," he interrupted. "It's Vice Principal George. I think he's on to you."

I nodded and tried to ignore the sudden feeling of my guts churning and bubbling inside me like percolating hot coffee.

"Yeah, I thought so," I said. "He's been on my case lately."

"It's worse than that, though, Mac. He came to me yesterday and asked for the key to this bathroom. He said he's been trying to get in here, and he wanted me to unlock it for him. I told him it was closed for health reasons, and he said he didn't care."

I shook my head. This couldn't be happening. Not now. Not with all the business I had to take care of. I needed my office. I didn't think I could organize this size of operation anywhere else.

"What did you say? Did you give him the key?" I asked.

He shook his head. "No. I told him I hadn't been in here in a while and so didn't know where the key was.

But he called me out. He said he saw some 'troublemakers' in here the other day. He told me that I had to bring him every copy of the key that I could find by the end of school today or I'd be fired. I'm sorry, Mac . . . but I have to do it. My kids . . ."

"I know," I said. "It's okay."

But it wasn't okay. Not at all. I felt like dropping to the ground and crying. I wanted to kick and scream and throw a tantrum like I sometimes saw little kids do in grocery stores when their moms didn't buy them candy. But I knew that wouldn't get me anywhere. It never did when I was that age either.

"That's not all, though, Mac. That's not even the worst of it," the janitor said.

"You're kidding, right? I just can't see how this can get worse."

"He said he was going to change the lock on the bathroom. He said he had reason to believe that a student had a key."

"But you'll get me a copy of the new key?"

The janitor smiled, but it was one of the saddest smiles I'd ever seen. "I'm afraid not, Mac. Dr. George said he was going to have a private locksmith make the change and that he'd be the only person with a key. No one is getting in and out of that bathroom except for Dr. George."

Now I wasn't just upset—I was angry. I'd worked so hard for this office, and I wasn't about to let some crusty old Suit on a power trip take it away. Dr. George was going to be sorry he'd ever called me into his office and messed with my business.

"Sorry again, buddy. I just wanted you to know so you could get anything out of here that you don't want found. I'd try to do it before school ends today if at all possible, because after school I'm going to deliver the old keys to Dr. George."

I nodded. But how could we even do that? We couldn't transport a desk and all the chairs and our Books and the cashbox and the DVRs and everything else while school was in session. Even in this wing of the school, we'd probably get caught. Besides, what would I do with my desk even if we got it out of the bathroom? Stash it in my locker? I almost grinned at the thought of all of us trying to slam the desk into my hopelessly tiny locker until it was nothing but a shattered mess of steel and wood.

Then I had an idea. Perhaps Victor, Vince's older brother, could park his truck outside the East Wing door after school. Then we could just pile up everything and haul it out and into the back of the truck in a few quick trips and take it to Vince's trailer until we figured out something else.

"Do you think you might be able to delay Dr. George

in his office when you drop off the keys? Just for like fifteen minutes?"

"I can try, Mac, but I can't promise any specific amount of time. My job is really on the line here. Old Georgie is really angry about all of this."

"We'll take whatever time we can get."

"Ready, lift!"

Vince and I took deep breaths and lifted either side of my desk.

We stumbled along awkwardly toward the bathroom door. It was 3:04. We had no more than three minutes to get all our stuff out of here and into Victor's truck. Fred was posted at the end of the hallway as an advance lookout. He had Victor's cell phone just in case.

I was supposed to be in detention at that very minute, but I doubted that Mr. Daniels would even notice that I didn't show. Besides, any punishment I got from missing detention would definitely be better than George finding all of my business materials.

Joe opened the door for us, and we shuffled out. Victor held open the door to the school, and we moved into the entryway and set down the desk. Joe came in behind us with a stack of plastic chairs.

"What are we waiting for?" he asked, peering out through the glass doors.

"Victor, go make sure there's nobody around. Stealing school property is a pretty serious offense; we shouldn't take any chances."

Victor ran outside and looked around the side of the building. He came back within view and gave us a thumbs-up.

"Let's go," I said.

Vince and I carried the desk outside, and Joe followed with the chairs. We lifted it all quickly and carefully into the back of Victor's small pickup. One trip down, one to go.

"Okay, let's just go get the cashbox and my Books and stuff, and . . . Joe, what is it?" I asked.

In the middle of my sentence he'd pulled out his phone, and now he looked as if he was about to pass out.

He held out the phone so I could read the screen.

gorge comin rite now :O

The text was from Fred.

"What should we do, Mac?" Joe asked.

Victor strung together a list of words that would have gotten him expelled instantly if he still went to school there.

"We have time, let's go," I said, and ran toward the bathroom.

The others followed. It never even entered my mind that we *didn't* have time to quickly grab all of our Books and my cashbox and the security camera DVR. I needed that stuff too badly. Without our Books we'd be lost. Plus, there was a pretty nice chunk of cash in the Tom Petty cashbox still hidden inside the trash can.

But we were too late.

As we entered the school, we practically ran right into Dr. George, his face so red and sweaty that it almost looked greasy instead of old and dry and crusty. A small man wearing black-framed glasses and a gray jump-suit stood next to him. The guy had a tool belt strung with long thin metal rods, sticks, keys, locks, and other assorted tools that I didn't recognize.

The locksmith.

"Hey, look who's here?" Dr. George said. "I knew it."

I turned just in time to see that Victor was already back outside, and Joe and Vince were right behind him. I joined in on the getaway.

I heard Dr. George blubbering behind me. "Hey, you can't . . . Get back here!"

I kept running.

When I got outside, Victor was already in the truck and Vince was getting into the passenger seat. In one high, graceful jump Joe hopped into the back of the truck's cab with the desk. I ran up behind the truck, jumped onto the bumper, and climbed into the cab just as Victor hit the gas pedal.

I looked back at the school in time to see Dr. George step outside. He stood calmly and watched us go. I saw him go back inside just before we turned the corner and drove out of view.

Chapter 19

Wednesday—Joe's House

"**W**hat are we going to do? What are we going to do?" Joe kept saying as he paced frantically back and forth across his backyard.

He was usually the calm one.

"But what if he finds the Books? We'll be expelled for sure, Mac," Joe said. "I mean, the stuff we've done that's documented in those things, like selling test answers and completed homework and prewritten research papers? Oh jeez, and the whole SMART thing! Oh man, oh man, forget expulsion; we might go to juvie for this stuff!"

He was having a breakdown. It was hard to watch. I'd never even seen the guy break a sweat before, and now here he was pacing around, talking to himself like a crazy person. I kept expecting him to, like, strip off all his clothes and go running around the neighborhood yelling stuff like, "Don't feed the bison! Hey, you! I said don't feed the bison!"

The worst part was that he was right. We'd be expelled for sure once George found the contents of the trash can. And this couldn't have happened at a worse time. If all the other stuff in the books wasn't enough to get us expelled, the documentation about the SMART operation surely would.

We stored my desk and chairs in Joe's toolshed and then thanked Victor for his help with a ten-dollar bill. Then we sat in Joe's backyard trying to figure out what we were going to do. Well, I tried to think of what we were going to do, Joe freaked out, and Vince just kept rambling on and on about stuff his grandma might say at this moment. Which I wasn't really finding all that funny just then.

"Joe, calm down, okay?" I said. "He won't find the Books if they're not there to find."

"Mac! They *are* there!"

"I know, I know. What I mean is they *won't* be. If he hasn't found them yet, which is a possibility, we'll just have to go in and get them."

Vince was on his feet now, nodding. "Yeah, I like it."

"How are we going to get in? Dr. George is the only one with a key," Joe said.

"Come on, Joe. You sound like you're talking about one of those video games where you always need to find the red keycard to get through the red door or whatever. This is real life. There are other ways to get into places besides with keys," I said. "We'll just get Tyrell's help again, like yesterday."

That night Joe, Vince, and I broke into the school. Well, is it still considered breaking in if you have a key? The janitor may have had to turn in his key to the bathroom, but I still had my key to the East Wing entrance.

We brought Tyrell with us for help doing the rest.

The four of us grouped outside the bathroom door in the dark hallway. There was no moon; the only light at all was the starlight sneaking in through the East Wing entrance's windows. We whispered even though the school was most likely empty at this time of the evening.

"Do your thing," I said to Tyrell.

He took out his lock-pick tool and unlocked the bathroom door. He gave a light push, and the door creaked open a few feet. I reached for the light switch as we walked in, but Tyrell grabbed my arm. He shook his head slowly and held up a flashlight. It clicked on and a pale orange beam hit the floor.

"This light will be very hard to notice through the window," he said, nodding at the high window at the end of the bathroom.

This kid seriously thought of everything.

We grouped around the trash can as Tyrell carefully removed the lid. He shined the flashlight in first and then dug his arm inside. My throat locked up, and it felt like I was choking on my own tongue. I was so ready to breathe a sigh of relief. I was ready for him to remove the Books and the cashbox and return them safely to me, their rightful owner.

But then he removed his arm, empty handed, and turned to face me.

"Mac, it's empty," he said.

I just about hit the floor. I swayed, and my vision glossed over like I was wearing dirty goggles. I finally remembered to breathe and regained my balance, but not passing out only made it worse, because then I had to face the truth: it was over. We'd all be expelled for sure.

I expected Joe to freak out again like he had earlier, but he didn't. Nobody did. We all just stood there staring at each other. It was as if we were all afraid to open our mouths for fear of puking all over the floor. I knew I probably would.

After confirming that the DVRs were gone, too, we

slowly oozed out of the bathroom, not even trying to stay low anymore. The cameras were the only thing left, but without DVRs to transmit to, they were basically worthless.

Tyrell relocked the door with his gadget, and I plopped down with my back against the wall. The others joined me. I didn't have the energy to ride my bike home just yet. This was worse than my business being shut down. This was probably the worst thing that could ever have happened. I didn't know how I could even face my parents. Expulsion was like the mark of death on a school transcript, or so I'd been told all my life anyways. But even worse than getting expelled, it meant the end of my business here at this school. It would probably even be the end of my business altogether, because the thought of starting over from scratch at a new school made me ill.

How long would it be before Dr. George axed us? Tomorrow? Two days? A week?

"Anybody want to hear what my grandma might say right now if she were here?" Vince said, but that funny glow that was usually in his eyes was completely gone.

Nobody said anything.

"She'd say, 'We're all really—' "

"Ahhh!" I yelled, cutting him off. "Screw this!"

I stood up and kicked the wall. I wasn't sure if I

thought it would buckle and crumble like a cracker, but it didn't. My toes felt like they had just gotten run over by a steamroller. I grabbed my foot and hopped up and down on one leg. Vince actually managed to laugh a little bit.

I noticed they were all looking at me, expecting me to say something else. But the fact was right then I didn't know what else to say. Vince's grandma was probably right about our situation just then. We were all pretty much doomed. Well, I'm pretty sure that her saying had a lot more swearwords in it than mine, but it meant the same thing either way.

Chapter

Thursday—Gymnasium

At baseball practice the next evening after school it was hard to focus. Basically we catchers kept trying to catch the pitchers but spent a lot of our time chasing down baseballs that were bouncing all over the junior high gym. I missed way more blocks than usual.

But in my case I had an excuse. Honestly, I was pretty surprised that I was even still a student at that point. Because all day had passed in a blur, with me expecting to get called down to Dr. George's office to get expelled at any minute. But it never happened. The day passed like any other, except for the fact that for the first time I had no business to run. Without an office there wasn't much I could do.

I'd barely even noticed all the kids that came up to me that day asking when we'd be open again and stuff. And plenty of kids were still super happy about the SMART stunt I'd pulled off. They kept trying to pay me, right in the middle of the hall, but I didn't take any of the money. I didn't do business outside my office, and I couldn't change that rule just because I didn't have an office anymore. Anyway, I was more popular than I'd ever been, which was kind of ironic considering I was at my lowest point professionally. Once George read those books or watched the DVR footage, I could kiss the school and all my friends good-bye.

At the end of practice Kjelson announced that he would be bringing in a few batting cages for us next week. It was time to see who could hit. Then we were dismissed. Vince and I decided to stick around to see if we could get a better read on Mr. Kjelson. If nothing else, maybe I could still help Hannah out with her problem.

"So, Coach," I said as he gathered up baseballs. "Why did you decide to come to our school to teach anyway?"

"Well, I was just looking for a change, that's all," he said.

"After getting teacher of the year at Oaks Crossing?" Vince prodded.

He looked at us funny but then just sighed. "This

school was desperate for a science teacher, and they made an offer I couldn't refuse."

He'd just used one of my favorite phrases. For a teacher he was definitely one of the coolest adults I'd met. Which is why I was getting more and more convinced that Hannah had to be telling the truth because Mr. K. was almost too good to be true.

I decided to press my luck.

"So it didn't have anything to do with Hannah Carol, then?"

His eyes narrowed instantly. That same odd look came over his face just like the last time I'd asked.

"Why do you keep asking about her? Did she say something to you two about me? Is that it? How do you know Hannah anyway? You're a little young to be friends with her, aren't you?"

"Why would she say something to us about you?" I asked.

"Well, because she—" He stopped, suddenly looking as if he hadn't meant to say even that much. "You still didn't answer my question. Why are you asking me about her?"

It almost seemed like he was getting angry now. Which was uncomfortable, because I'd never seen him like this before. It was like getting to see the dark side of the moon for the first time and discovering that it was covered with a St. Louis Cardinals logo. For a Cubs fan that's a pretty unpleasant thought.

I wanted to press him further because I clearly had him shaken. But I was almost afraid to; it seemed likely that pressing this further might get Hannah in even more trouble. In fact he probably might have already figured out that she'd told us about how he was treating her. Plus, I was pretty sure I'd just seen all I needed to know.

They were both waiting for me in the living room when I walked through the door after getting home from practice. My mom sat in the recliner, her eyes red from crying. My dad stood behind her; his jaw clenched so tightly, it looked like he was trying to crush coal into diamonds with his teeth.

"What's up, Moms and Pops?" I asked with a grin.

I tried to play it off innocently, but I knew this meant something. And I knew what it was. Dr. George wouldn't talk to us first about expulsion. He would contact our parents directly. Of course that was why we hadn't gotten called into his office today. I wanted to punch myself for being so stupid.

"Sit down," my dad managed to say without unclenching his jaw.

I sat down on the sofa. I tried to smile, to play it cool,

but I couldn't bring myself to do it. Not when my life was basically over. Now I'd have to discontinue my business, find a new school, and who knew if Vince would even get into the same school as me. Plus, I'd probably gotten Joe and Fred and Tyrell expelled, too. It was my fault that their lives would basically be ruined.

"What do you have to say for yourself?" my dad said.

"About what?"

He chortled and shook his head. He almost smiled, he was so angry. That was never a good sign.

"How many times have I told you that school comes first? Huh? I always say you need to stop running off and playing your little games with Vincent, but did you ever listen?" he shouted.

"School does come fir—"

"Don't you dare even say it, Christian!" my dad yelled.

My mom just sat there staring at the floor. She shook her head and held back more tears.

We sat in silence for a while. Then my mom finally spoke.

"Why didn't you tell us you were having problems, Christian? There are ways we could have helped. There are . . . *ways*." She said this as if whatever ways she meant were not legal.

I was confused now. What the heck did that mean?

My dad sighed, looking sort of calm for the first time.

"What your mother is trying to say is it's not a bad thing to have troubles in school, but you have to tell somebody. There are a lot of . . . *conditions* that can cause these problems. If you were struggling so badly, why didn't you come to us for help?"

Now I was sure I was losing my mind. I always did well in school. School's a piece of cake.

"Okay, Dad, I'm really sorry, but I honestly have no idea what you guys are talking about. What did I do?"

This only made my mom start crying again. I thought I heard her say, "Doesn't even know," through her sobs.

"Christian, we got your SMART scores back today. You . . . well, you didn't really *meet the standards*."

"That's what this is about?" I said. I was still in too much shock to realize what that meant because my first reaction was relief.

"Don't you even care?" my dad said, anger seeping back into his voice.

"Of course I do. I just, I thought it was something really bad, you know?"

"This is really bad!" my dad yelled. "You didn't meet graduation standards, Christian. Do you know what that means? It means you failed so badly that you likely will be held back. It means you will have to take sixth grade all over again next year!"

Then it finally hit me how impossible what he was

telling me actually was. There was no way. I'd fixed my own answer sheet myself, personally, on Tuesday. I'd given myself a near perfect score. How could this even be possible?

"Are you sure I failed? I mean . . . there's just no way!" I said. "Besides, I have all As in school. How could they fail me for one bad test?"

My dad shook his head like I wouldn't understand. But he tried to explain anyways.

"Yes, we're sure, Christian. There's no mistaking it; you didn't even get a fifty percent. It's a new thing, Christian. The state government thought that our schools needed higher accountability. Do you know what that word means? Too many kids who can't even read have been graduating from high school, and everybody is ignoring it. So now they implemented these new tests to make sure that all kids are getting the education they need to succeed in life. Your grades don't matter so much. All that your As mean is that Mr. Skari is not doing his job well enough. This test proves that."

"But Mr. Skari is a good teacher," I said.

"Apparently not. Why else would you fail this test so miserably yet still have decent grades in his class? You didn't even test *close* to your grade level, Christian!"

This made my mom sob again. I guess parents really hate learning that their kid is stupid.

"Yeah, well, that just sucks," I said. "The test was rigged. Mr. Skari is a good teacher." Of course I didn't say I *knew* it had to be rigged somehow since I'd had the answer key sitting on my lap when I filled in my scores.

My mom jumped at this, and my dad shook his head.

"Don't use that kind of language in our house, Christian. Now get upstairs. You're grounded for the rest of the year, buddy. You will do homework and study every night from the time you get home till the time you go to bed. Upstairs, now!"

I went upstairs. There was no point arguing this. I lay in bed for a while trying to figure out how this was even possible. I had changed my answers myself; there was just no way. Unless someone, like, broke back into the administration offices later that night and re-changed all of the answers or something. But who would do that?

Then it hit me. There already was someone trying to take down the whole school. We'd figured that out already. There were the lunches and the poop in the lockers. . . . This was just the latest part of their plan. I didn't know how they were doing it and I didn't know why, but that had to be it. And the worst part was that they were succeeding.

Chapter  21

Friday—Mac's Locker

I t became pretty clear quickly the next day that I wasn't the only one who'd failed. As soon as I stepped inside the school, kids had been glaring at me in a way I'd never seen before. And then I got to my locker and found the notes.

I could read only a few of them before I had to stop. I'd gotten plenty of thank-you notes over the years and a few rogue threats and hate notes. But never before at one time had I gotten so many notes with the words "hate you," and "liar," and "jerk," and "backstabber," and on and on. My locker had been stuffed full of them already, and it wasn't even 8:15 yet. Some of the notes were so vulgar, they'd have made my mom pass out. And some were so bad that they had swearwords on them I'd never even heard of before.

I saw Vince heading over, and he looked pretty sick. Kids weren't looking at him any more kindly than they were at me. In fact one kid tried to trip Vince as he got near me. He didn't quite fall, but he did stumble and drop one of his books. I picked it up.

"What happened, Mac?"

I shook my head.

"Someone had to have shown up after us and messed with the answer sheets," Vince said.

I nodded. I couldn't even talk to him. I wasn't mad at him of course. I was just too mad in general to even get any words out. I think he must have understood this, because he just patted me on the shoulder in a friendly way.

"It's all right, Mac. We'll figure this out. We always do," he said before heading off toward his classroom.

I nodded as I started toward my own, but I didn't feel much better. Nor did I agree with him. I was pretty sure that this time we really were screwed.

As the day went on, it became clear that this was a big deal. Mr. Skari looked like a hollow piece of wood rather than a teacher, or even a live human being. He just gave us a really long reading assignment and then slumped behind his desk. It kind of broke me to see him so defeated. Because I knew this wasn't his fault. He didn't deserve this; none of us did.

By morning recess I'd heard plenty of rumors. It sounded like pretty much the whole school had failed. And a lot of kids seemed to think that the whole school was going to be shut down soon. Others didn't think that was possible; they said that the school would simply bring in more administrators or make us all stay until four o'clock every day for the rest of the year.

I met up with Joe and Fred and Vince down by the new playground, where I knew we'd be able to talk business mostly undisturbed. But kids kept coming down there to yell at us for ruining their lives and call me a snake and all kinds of other horrible stuff. I'd never felt lower or more embarrassed in my life. Or more angry.

So that's how our meeting started, with me stomping around throwing a fit, basically.

After I'd stomped around enough to calm down to the point where I could actually get words out of my mouth without cursing, I faced the others.

"We're not just going to give up. We're not just going to roll over and die. We need to make a plan. We need to take control back. First let's get ourselves a new office. Not to take customers just yet but merely a place where we can brainstorm, figure out what to do, and take care of any outstanding business. So at lunch meet me by the old truck tires. We're going to set up shop right where it all started. Are you all sticking with me?"

"Count me in," Vince said.

Joe hesitated but only for a second or two. "Me, too."

Fred nodded.

At this point it would have been appropriate for us to all group into a circle, put our hands together, and then say, "Go team!" while throwing our arms into the air. But I decided that would be really lame, so instead we just headed back to class.

We found more resistance than I'd expected when we met at the truck tires after lunch. One of the two huge tires buried in the gravel on the grade school side of the playground had been my office years ago, but most of the younger kids didn't know that. And they weren't all that willing to give up their favorite play spot. Not to me, the kid who had just supposedly screwed over everybody.

"We'll tell on you," one of them said with his chest jutted out like he was Superman or something. He was a little first grader with dirt-filled boogers running down his face.

"I'll just move him," Joe said, stepping forward.

"Wait," I said, blocking him with my arm, "if we do that, he'll just tell on us. Kids these days don't follow the same code of ethics that we used to. They're all squealers."

I moved closer to the snot-nosed first grader. I reached into my pocket, and he flinched, looking intimidated for the first time. I pulled out a dollar bill and waved it in front of his face.

"If I give you this, will you agree to play somewhere else for a while?"

"A dollar?" he said.

I nodded. Little kids loved money; you could always count on that much.

"What the heck am I supposed to do with a crappy dollar? I can't buy anything for a buck," he sneered. His little pack of buddies laughed.

"Get out of here, geeks," one of them said.

At his age I would have done just about anything for a buck. I'm pretty sure I once ate a live spider the size of a nickel for fifty cents. Yet here this little kid was, laughing at me, his snot-encrusted face disrespecting me at my school.

"Don't you know who I am?" I asked.

The kid thought it over. "Some loser who likes to play in tires."

Joe made a move as if he was going to pound the kid into the ground, but I stopped him.

"I'm the one who took down Staples," I said. "Remember when that all happened? That was me. I took him down."

The kid's eyes widened. He looked impressed and scared for the first time. But then his little punk smirk returned. "No you're not. You're a liar. You're too small and dumb to take out Staples. And my sister failed her SMART because of you."

I shook my head and backed up to whisper some instructions to Joe. He ran off, and we waited, watching the little first-grade punk and his buddies climb all over my new/old office.

After a few minutes Joe returned with a small kid in Dockers khaki slacks and a sweater vest with reindeer on it. His hair was combed neatly and tightly across his skull, leaving a perfectly straight part-line running across his head like from the blade of a knife. He calmly approached us, and the little first graders dismounted the tires, looking truly terrified for the first time.

Even these little kids weren't too young to know who Kitten was. Kitten was easily the most notoriously dangerous bully in school history. Which was pretty impressive considering that he had only gone to this school for a few years. Everybody, young and old—even you at this point—knew the dangers of crossing Kitten.

"You know who this is, right?" I said.

The little first-grade ringleader nodded slowly.

"We're taking these tires for my new office. And if you tattle on us, then you'll have to deal with my good pal Kitten here. Understand?"

The little kids stood there staring with wide, white eyes.

I gave a nod to Kitten. He took a few steps forward, and the flock of first graders scrambled. They ran off in all directions, some of them so frantically that they fell several times before making their actual getaway.

I shook Kitten's hand, pressing a five-dollar bill into it.

He nodded and wandered off without saying a word.

"Nice work," Vince said.

"It was all Kitten," I said.

Vince shrugged.

We decided to set up my office in the far tire, which was actually just fifteen feet or so from the sidewalk and the edge of school property. It was a much tighter fit than before because I was almost a foot taller, but it still worked. It would hopefully only be temporary anyways.

The first thing I did was have Joe fetch Tyrell for me. I asked him to trail Dr. George, to see if he could figure out why we hadn't been expelled yet. There was at least a chance that he hadn't gotten around to reviewing all the stuff he'd confiscated from my office, due to the SMART mess, which I'm sure was creating a bunch of extra work for him.

What I didn't expect, though, was for Tyrell to show up with news so quickly. He stopped by the truck tire at the start of late recess.

"Tyrell, you have news already?"

"That I do, Mac." He grinned at me. I knew already that this would be a good visit. This kid was amazing.

"Let's have it, then."

"It's all in Dr. George's office. Every last one of your and Vince's Books and the cashbox and the DVRs. He's still got it all stashed in his office."

"Do you know where in his office?"

"Yeah, he keeps it all in his desk drawer. I don't think there's any way we can get the stuff during school hours, but after hours . . ."

"What about tonight? Can we get it tonight?" I asked.

"We?" Tyrell said, and then shook his head. "Mac, I got this. You don't even need to be there. Plus, I thought you were grounded?"

"I am, but that's never stopped me from getting out in the past. My parents aren't the issue. No, I'm going with. If you get caught, I can't let you take the fall for this alone. Besides, I like a little fieldwork from time to time."

"Sure thing, Mac. Can you meet me in the parking lot here around eight o'clock?"

"No problem. Thanks, Tyrell. Seriously." I held out my hand.

He shook it and then pocketed the twenty-dollar bill that I had handed him. He nodded at me and was gone before I could even blink.

Word must have spread that I'd been hanging out in the truck tire that day because Hannah came to see me not long after Tyrell left.

"Wow, moving up in the world, I see," she said as she looked around the inside of the tire.

"Hey, we take what we can get, okay?"

"Wow, relax. I'm just joking with you," she said with that one grin she has. It's like only half of her mouth is smiling and the other half doesn't move at all, like she's hiding something.

"I'm still working on your problem, if that's why you're here. We've had some complications. But it's on my agenda. You can understand we've been a little busy lately."

She nodded. She seemed more complacent than usual. "Okay. I suppose I can handle one more day of detention and inhumane cruelty. But do you think you could do another favor for me?"

I wanted to say, "No, you're more trouble than you're worth." But at the same time I didn't want her to leave. I liked this calmer version of Hannah, like in gym class the other day. Besides, what kind of business owner would say something like that?

"Depends," I said.

She laughed. Her rattlesnake laugh was growing on me; I hated to admit that to myself.

"Well, obviously you know that I failed my SMART, being that I heard you were supposedly fixing the test for us. But whatever went wrong there, I know you probably tried your best. Anyway, I was just wondering, you know, like when you do whatever it is that you do to solve something like that, that you could keep me in mind, too."

"Yeah, no problem. I can do that," I said, even though I wasn't so sure I could fix this one for anybody.

"Well, I guess that came out wrong. What I meant to say was if you need my help, just ask," she said, smiling her half smile.

"Okay, I will," I said. "Thanks, Hannah."

That I had not been expecting. But it was nice to know that she at least, of all people, still had my back.

I watched her leave. On her way out I saw her stop

and visit with Vince. He said something, and she laughed much harder than she had when she was in here with me. She even reached out and squeezed his arm. I wanted to run outside and yell at Vince to get back to work. Seriously, what was with him? This was business time not social hour.

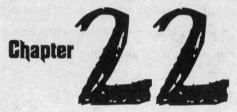

Chapter 22

Friday—Bedroom

"**A**re you sure you don't want me to come with?" Vince asked as we played video games in my room that evening.

"Yeah. What would be the point of putting another of us at risk? It's not going to take more than one or two of us to get this done. You just stay at home and see what you can figure out regarding the SMART problem."

"Okay," he said, but I think he knew as well as I did that there might not be much we could do there.

Someone had messed with the answer sheets later that night, and we couldn't change that. Not unless Vince could ever get his time machine to actually work like time machines were supposed to—you know, as in going backward and forward in time. A few years ago Vince had drawn up plans to build a time machine. As soon as I saw his list of construction materials, I told him he was crazy. His so-called plans called for a large "coffin-sized" Tupperware container; seven lawn gnomes all with various differing height, weight, beard length, etc., etc.; a large black Magic Marker with no ink left; three down pillows—two white, the third "yellowing"; and—here's the kicker and the reason Vince claims the time machine wasn't working properly—a large English-speaking badger with an IQ of exactly 134. Amazingly Vince rounded up all that other stuff, but until he found that badger, he claimed his time machine would only function at one setting: moving forward in time at regular speed. Anyways, unless Vince found that badger in the next few days, there wasn't any way I could change the scores back to the way we had them.

"Hey, I've got a Cubs question for you," he said.

I wasn't really in the mood for his question, but he'd for sure never let me forget it if I tried to back out now.

"Okay, go," I said.

"Who were the last and first Cubs pitchers to hit a home run in the postseason?"

I nodded. It was a tricky question. I guessed he wanted me to think that it was probably Carlos Zambrano as the last and then some really old-school guy from before World War I for the first. But he'd underestimated me yet again.

"The first was way, way, way back in . . . ," I started and saw his eyes light up, "1984, when Rick Sutcliffe did it."

He slumped forward, disappointed.

"The last one to do it was Kerry Wood in 2003. And those are the only two to ever do it."

"Nicely done, Mac. I thought you might think it was Zambrano."

I grinned at him and gave a shrug that said, *I can't help it that I'm smarter than you.*

"Ah, Boris Yeltsin anyways," Vince said.

I laughed. That was *usually* what his Grandma said instead of swearwords, except when she was in church, of course. Vince had adopted it pretty quickly as his favorite swearword.

We finished our game, and then Vince left by going out the window since, really, he wasn't supposed to be over in the first place, considering that I was grounded.

"Good luck tonight," he said as he left.

I nodded and waved good-bye. I'd need it.

Sneaking out of my house was easy. Whether or not my parents would eventually find out was more the question. I went out the window just like Vince had, a classic escape route. I placed pillows under my sheets like I was already sleeping in case they came into my room, another classic decoy. I know, way to be original, right? But the thing is, those moves are classics for a reason.

Tyrell was already waiting for me in the parking lot when I got there. Though I didn't see him until I practically tripped over him.

He was wearing all black, including black sunglasses to keep the whites of his eyes hidden. He'd been crouching in the shadows of the school Dumpster, but with all that black I didn't see him even after he spoke to me.

"Mac, watch out," he said.

I dropped to the ground. "Who's there?"

"It's me," he said, tapping my shoulder.

I jumped because I didn't expect him to be that close to me already.

"You're gonna kill me one of these days, seriously. A guy's heart can only take so much."

"Sorry, Mac. We all don't sound like a stampede of elephants when we're sneaking around."

"Am I really that bad?" I asked.

He laughed. "Not *that* bad. Are you ready?"

I nodded, and we were off. We got in through the East Wing entrance, which I still had a key to. The halls were almost pitch black, but somehow Tyrell guided us right to the administration offices without so much as a keychain flashlight. The kid was like a chameleon, *and* he could see in the dark.

This was where it would get a little trickier.

"You're wearing gloves, right?" he whispered.

I held up my hands. I'd found a pair of my mom's black knit, stretch gloves. The only ones I owned were big clumsy winter gloves that would have made my hands so useless, they might as well have been horse hooves.

Tyrell nodded an approval. He dug inside his bag and took out his lock-pick gun. I turned on his flashlight with the soft orange glow.

"Point it at the lock for me," he said.

Within seconds we were inside the administration office area. It was dark except for a faint red light coming from the power strip by the secretary's desk. We worked our way over to Dr. George's office, and Tyrell did his lock-pick thing and then we were in. Easy as pie.

We moved in the dark to behind Dr. George's desk. Tyrell had said before that he knew exactly where George kept all of our stuff. He pulled the handle to the lowest, largest drawer. It didn't budge.

"Locked," he whispered.

"So use your gun thingy on it," I said.

He shook his head. "That won't work on this kind of lock. It's too small and it doesn't use a pin tumbler. I'll have to do this old-school."

"Whatever. Just hurry up," I said.

In the dim glow of the orange-light flashlight I could see him grinning as he dug in his pack for something. "What's wrong, Mac? Getting nervous?" he asked.

"Of course. If we get caught in here, we're dead." After I said this, I realized that that was true if we didn't get our stuff back as well.

Tyrell didn't respond but moved smoothly and quickly as he took out a small pouch from his bag and removed several long skinny rods with jagged, flat ends. And then another thin piece of metal shaped like an L. I shined the pale orange light on the desk's lock as he went to work.

Within a few minutes I heard a small click, and he pulled out the heavy drawer. I had the light shining inside before the drawer was even all the way out. With my luck as of late I expected to find a drawer full of nothing but detention slips and poisonous spiders. But there wasn't either.

The entire drawer contained nothing but my small metal lockbox and a few notebooks that I recognized as our Books and the two DVR receivers. My hands started shaking, I was so excited to see that stuff.

I took the key to the lockbox out of my pocket and unlocked it. My cash was still stuffed safely inside. So maybe George hadn't had a chance to go through all of this stuff just yet? I couldn't help but grin. Even if he had, now that he didn't have the proof in his possession anymore, he'd have a really hard time being able to get us expelled. In school even the top Suits needed proof— they couldn't just do whatever they wanted. There were still procedures and stuff. I took the discs out of the DVRs and put the DVRs back, seeing as how we couldn't carry the recorders back on our bikes. Then I relocked the cashbox and stuffed it, the DVR discs, and my Books inside my backpack.

"All ready to go?" I asked Tyrell.

He shut and relocked the drawer, put away his tools, and gave me a thumbs-up. We stood up to leave, and then I noticed a few stacks of SMART booklets lying on Dr. George's desk. I stopped and flipped open the top test and shined my pale orange beam at it.

"Mac, what are you doing? We have to go. This was supposed to be in and out," Tyrell whispered.

"I just need to look at this," I said.

On the very top of the pile was a sticky with this scribbled on it: *Confiscated from Kjelson's room.* I could tell from the big calendar on his desk that the note was in Dr. George's writing. So George had found all of these in Kjelson's room.

Inside the front cover of the first booklet was a printed sheet with graphs and lines thrown up all over it like a seafood lunch buffet gone wrong. On each pile of booklets there were more Post-it notes. Some were labeled: *Originals?* Others: *Altered stage 1.* There was also a pile for each grade level labeled: *xth grade altered,* and another pile for each grade labeled: *xth grade actual.* The writing on these notes I thought I recognized as Mr. Kjelson's from his handwritten welcome notes he'd sent to all of us who'd tried out for baseball. There were even more piles, too, as well as fifteen or twenty used, bloated lab notebooks, but I didn't really need to see anything more. I'd seen plenty.

And I didn't even get any time to absorb the shock because Tyrell was tugging at my sleeve and pointing to his ear.

I listened. I heard a faint creak from behind Dr. George's door.

Somebody was right outside in the administration offices area.

Then the distinct sound of a key sliding into the doorknob lock on Dr. George's door snapped us into action. Well, I still stood there like an idiot, but Tyrell grabbed my arm and pulled me underneath Dr. George's desk.

That probably seems like a horrible place to hide. It probably was, but it was all we had time for. Besides, Dr. George's desk was massive, the size of an aircraft carrier, so there was plenty of room for us to squeeze into the very back corner behind the empty trash can. The front of the desk was solid, so the only way we'd be detected was if the intruder looked under the desk or sat in the chair and stretched his legs out really far.

The door to the office opened with a high, faint creak and closed with a loud thud.

The lights flickered on as the intruder coughed and any doubts of who it was disappeared. Dr. George's coughs sounded like rusty roller skates rolling over rusty nails on top of a rusty sheet of metal being carried by two rust-colored hyenas. I clutched my bag tightly in my arms. Even if he found us, there was no way I was letting him put his crusty old hands on my stuff again.

Dr. George pulled out his chair, and I held my breath. He sat down without so much as a pause and pulled himself closer so that his legs were only six inches from our faces. And the worst part was that Dr. George was wearing shorts. He must have just come from the gym or something. I don't know if you've ever seen old-man legs up close, but trust me, you don't ever want to.

It was weird to see Dr. George in shorts and not just because it was still winter. I'd only ever seen him in suits. Somehow the shorts made him feel like less of a threat. More like an actual human and less like a Suit. But I knew it was dangerous to think that way. A grizzly bear wearing a pretty dress, angel wings, and a halo is still a grizzly bear, and it would still eat you if it were hungry enough.

Dr. George shuffled through some of the papers on his desk. I tried not to look at his gross, white legs too much, but I couldn't help it; it was like watching a gory horror movie. You knew it would gross you out, but you couldn't take your eyes away.

My legs were starting to cramp, and I wasn't sure how long I'd be able to stay still, neatly folded up under this desk like a shirt in a retail store.

Then Dr. George picked up his phone, and I heard his long crusty finger punching the keys.

"Hey, it's me," he said. "No, I know. Mr. Kjelson is definitely up to something regarding the SMARTs. . . . I'll get to the bottom of it. . . . No, don't do that. I'll take care of it. . . . Yeah, I'm already getting calls on it, and I have a meeting with some officials in a few days. . . . I don't know what he's trying to do, but I'll make sure he doesn't do any more damage than he's already done. Also, I just wanted to confirm the open school board meeting to discuss these serious school issues for next Tuesday night in the Olson Olson Theatre . . . Okay. I'll talk to you tomorrow, then."

Dr. George put the phone back on the cradle.

His one-way conversation raised even more questions

about Mr. Kjelson. But given all of the evidence, there probably weren't even any questions left. First there was the way Mr. Kjelson had acted about the SMARTs every time I brought them up. Then there was the fact that Vince and I had seen him at the school that night we'd altered the tests and he was headed toward the administration offices. Then there was all the stuff we'd just found and heard, piles of altered tests with Kjelson's writing all over them, and evidence that George believed Kjelson might have altered the tests in some way.

Maybe that's why Hannah had come to me for help with him? Maybe she knew what he was really up to and she didn't think I'd believe her, right along with every-body else? But the only question left was still why. Why would Kjelson do all of this? What exactly did he have against our school? Could he really be doing all of this just to make Hannah's life miserable? I wasn't sure, but it was clear I needed to have a chat with Hannah and then also probably confront Kjelson at some point. I may not have been able to change anything at this point, but not knowing why someone wanted to destroy our school would haunt me for the rest of my life if I didn't ever get answers. This whole thing was turning into a black hole, which is a thing that consumes all matter, something from which nothing can escape, and where no light can exist at all.

Dr. George's feet shuffled, and he grunted as he got up from the chair. He crossed the room slowly then stopped. I tensed up and then my leg bumped the trash can, which made a distinct noise that sounded like a bass drum in the empty and silent office.

George quickly started back for his desk, and I heard Tyrell gasp next to me. Tyrell almost never panicked, and so it was at that point that I knew we were really in trouble. We were as good as expelled now, even after all this, after the hope that we'd be okay.

Maybe we'd be worse than expelled. I mean, we broke into a locked office. I'm pretty sure kids had gone to juvie for less. Dr. George circled around the desk. I couldn't even breathe anymore, and it felt like my heart was trying to punish me for my stupid mistake, it was pounding against my ribs so hard. And I'm pretty sure it fractured one of them, my chest hurt so badly now.

George started bending over and then we all jumped, including George, as a loud alarm started ringing through the halls. I recognized it as the fire alarm. Dr. George jumped so bad that he hit his knee on his desk. He yelled and cursed, which was a lifesaver because I didn't think he heard me breathing so hard you'd think I'd just run a mile.

Dr. George bolted from the room: the light went out, and the door opened and slammed shut. I heard the faint noise of the door to the administration office opening and closing, and then there was only black and the piercing alarm ringing into our still-shocked brains.

I knew we needed to move fast because after George got the alarm turned off, there was a good chance he'd come back here.

"Let's go," I said to Tyrell.

In the very faint light I saw him nod.

Tyrell switched on the pale orange light, and I took that as my cue to crawl out from under the desk. Once we were both out, we ran to the door. Tyrell told me to wait while he went ahead to make sure the coast was clear.

He came back after a few moments. "Let's go."

We stayed low and moved quickly out of the office and then into the hallway. Tyrell indicated for me to be quiet and follow him. He led us to the north exit, which was actually a lot farther away than the south exit, but I figured Tyrell must have reason to believe that George had headed south.

We didn't see any signs of life as we moved through the dark hallways. Then after what seemed like a ten-mile hike even though it was really just like fifty yards, we were outside in the cold winter air. We still stayed low and quiet as we headed toward the bushes where we'd parked our bikes.

Right when we were passing the portables, a voice said, "Hey guys!"

I would have jumped if I hadn't recognized the voice so easily.

"What are you doing here?" I said.

Vince grinned at me. "I knew you'd need my help."

"You pulled that alarm?"

Vince just kept grinning. "I was watching the situation from the closet alcove near the library. I saw George head back and knew I had to do something."

Tyrell clapped Vince on the shoulder, pretty proud of his clever and quick actions. It was hard to impress Tyrell. I just shook my head, even more in awe of my best friend than I thought I could be.

"Well, thanks. You saved us. And we got all of our stuff back," I said, patting my backpack. "But I'm afraid we found even more than that."

Vince's smile faded.

I filled him in on the revelations about Kjelson. When I'd finished, Vince looked about as confused as I felt.

"We need to talk to Hannah, then," he said, referring to her offer to help us earlier that day. We both agreed that it seemed like she must know more than she was telling us. And just maybe that meant she could help us fix this somehow.

I nodded. "And then Kjelson. If we can figure out why

he wants to take down the school, maybe there's still time to stop him."

But I didn't think Vince believed those words any more than I did. They sounded even weaker coming out of my mouth than I thought they would. I thought we all knew there was little chance of fixing this anymore. But I knew one thing: giving up definitely wouldn't help, so I might as well hold on to that last string of hope we had left. It was just like the Cubs every year: everyone knows they don't have a chance, but they still give it their best.

Monday—West Side of the School

The first order of business for me the next school day was to find Hannah. I had to see if we could take her up on her offer to help us fix the SMART issue, which just so happened to also be the answer to her problem as well: Mr. Kjelson.

I went over it all in my head as we walked over to find her. Kjelson arrives at our school, and all the problems start shortly after. Then Vince and I see him sneaking around school with cages of hamsters and other lab animals just as we're getting reports of poop being planted in lockers. Then a student, Hannah, who apparently has known him longer than all of us, tells us he's crooked. Also, he gets dodgy every time we bring up the

SMARTs, and we just happen to see him hanging around the administration offices the very night we altered the answer sheets only to find out a few days later that all the tests failed. Then, to top it all off, we find direct evidence in George's office that Kjelson altered the tests and that even George is on to him. It was almost as easy as adding up two and two.

It was heartbreaking because Coach Kjelson had seemed like such a cool guy, and he was a Cubs fan. But then again, if a traitor like Mark Grace could be a Cub for close to ten years, then it was possible that there were some corrupt Cubs fans out there as well.

Joe, Vince, and I started our search for Hannah during early recess on the west side of the school, the place where most of the seventh and eighth graders hung out. And finding her actually wasn't nearly as hard as I thought it would be. But then again, she wasn't exactly hiding from us.

She was down near the skating rink. I tried to stay away from the skating rink as much as possible. It wasn't really a dangerous area of the school in terms of bullies, not like near the teeter-totters, which was pretty much skid row, but the skating rink was perhaps the most dangerous area in the school because that's where all of the eighth-grade girls hung out. Nobody knew for sure exactly what they did down there, but most believed they spent a lot of their time talking about different ways to make boys so confused they cried. Some kids also said the girls lit a bunch of scented candles and performed sacrifices on small animals to help them discover what the newest fashions would be and which boy would be the hottest one the next summer. That didn't seem too likely to me, but you never could know for sure when it came to girls. Because as I've said before, more than a few times: in school, girls are more dangerous than shotguns.

Hannah was with a small group of four girls. They were sitting in a row with their backs against the outside of the skating rink; none of them were wearing ice skates. They saw us coming from a mile away.

Hannah smiled warmly when she saw me, as if she was actually happy I'd come to see her. She looked more like a nice person and less like a poisonous snake at that moment than ever before.

"Hi, Mac," she said as we approached.

I nodded.

"This is that kid I told you about," she said to her friends, and they responded with giggles.

"Can I speak with you for a moment?" I asked, trying to keep my face from turning red.

"Sure."

I waited, and she just sat there looking at me with the sweetest smile I'd ever seen. I'd probably tell you it was *too* sweet if you asked me enough times.

"Um, in private," I said.

"That works two ways," she said, still grinning.

I nodded at Vince and Joe and they nodded back.

"Okay, let's go," I said to Hannah.

She got up and followed me around to the other side of the ice rink. Not all the way around to the other side but at least around the bend and out of earshot of our friends. She was still smiling when I turned to face her.

"What is it?" she asked.

"Take a guess," I said.

She raised her eyebrows and shook her head. Her dark hair swung across her face. "I don't know. You want to admit that you've fallen deeply and madly in love with me?"

I took a step back almost as if she'd slapped me in the face.

"No! I'm . . . Why would you think that?" I asked, again trying desperately to keep my face from turning red.

She started laughing. "You're really too easy, Mac."

I waited while she got it out of her system.

After she finally stopped laughing, I said, "You know what this is really about?"

For the first time her smile disappeared. "No, I really don't. What's wrong?"

"It's Kjelson. I think you were right about him all along. And I was wondering what you know about him that we don't. I mean, this goes way deeper than him just being mean to you; he's trying to take down the whole school!"

"What?" she said.

"Tell me right now what's really up with Mr. Kjelson," I demanded. "We need to know so we can take him down. This is bigger than just your thing right now. The future of the school is on the line!"

"Okay, first of all it's pronounced 'Chel-Sun,' not 'Kuh-Gel-Sun.' Second I already told you. . . ."

"No, you didn't tell me the real reason, okay?" I said, my voice rising more than I'd intended. "You need to tell me why you really want him out, or else I'll—"

"Hey, what's going on here?" some super-tan eighth grader asked as he approached us.

We both stopped and looked at him.

"Is this little punk hassling you? You want me to get rid of him?" His bangs were spiked up, and he wore a long-sleeved shirt under a short-sleeved polo with the collar raised around his neck like some sort of wall. And he had dimples in the sides of his face like giant caves in the sides of a mountain.

"Can't you see we're having a private conversation, Prince Charming?" Hannah said to the guy.

He flinched and took a step back. "Hey, I just thought . . ."

"Yeah, you just thought you'd come rescue the poor, defenseless little girl, right? I can take care of myself, Ditty Pop. Now leave us alone!"

Prince Charming put up his hands and backed away. "Okay, whatever. Jeez, sorry I tried to help."

"Hannah, listen to me, please?"

She didn't say anything. But she also didn't walk away.

"Look, I've got reason to believe that Mr. Kjelson is trying to get our school shut down forever, so I need to know what you know about him if we're going to have any chance to stop that from happening."

"That can't be right," she said.

"Well, it is. The thing is, I thought you were wrong. I thought that he was a great teacher and really cool guy. But then I started finding things out."

She shook her head. "No, this can't be right at all."

"I don't have time for any more stories, Hannah. I need to know what's going on or we're all going to get shipped off to other schools, maybe as soon as next week!"

Hannah looked uncertain at first, and I wasn't sure I

was ever going to get anything real out of her. But then I saw her will break like a stale wheat cracker. She let out this huge sigh, like she'd been holding her breath for a month.

"Mr. Kjelson is my dad."

I couldn't say anything. I basically stood there gaping at her like an idiot. That couldn't be right. She took my silence for what it was and then continued.

"I know, I know, our last names are different. Carol is my mom's last name, and I use it here at school. Anyway, we moved here earlier this year when my dad got this new job. He said it was 'an offer he couldn't refuse,' which I just rolled my eyes to at the time, of course."

After the disbelief hit me in the face and I reeled for a bit, I started to realize that they did kind of look alike. And it wasn't totally unbelievable. But then again, she had proven to be a pathological liar so far, and there were still details that didn't make any sense.

"But how could nobody know you're related? Why didn't he say so when I asked him about you? And most of all, why would you want your own dad fired?" The questions spilled out onto the grass between us like I'd eaten rotten questions for lunch or something.

"Nobody knows we're related because that's how I want it. At my old school, Oaks Crossing, everybody *loved* my dad. He was everybody's favorite teacher. Do you know what it's like to have kids like your dad more than you? I mean, parents and teachers are supposed to be dorks; everybody knows that. It was embarrassing. So I told him that if he was making me move to this dumb town and dumb school, then he couldn't let anyone know we were related. I was sick of just being known as Mr. Kjelson's weird daughter. Is that such a crime?"

"Well, not really, but that still doesn't explain why you wanted to get your own dad fired. . . . Is it because you found out he's trying to sabotage the school?"

"What? No! He'd never do anything like that; he loves this school. He always says it's way better than that snobby Oaks Crossing. I wanted him to get fired because I thought that if he lost his job, I could go back to my old school, my old friends. I guess I'm still kinda mad at him for moving me here, away from my old life."

I shook my head. That was why. *That* right there was why they say that in grade school, girls are more dangerous than shotguns. They can go after you for the smallest things. And whatever it is they're thinking at any given moment, it doesn't ever seem to make sense to anybody but them.

"But didn't you just say that you hated your old school because everybody liked your dad better?" I asked.

"Well, obviously not, like, *everybody* everybody.

I was exaggerating for effect; I still had friends and everything."

"Oh," was all I could think of to say back.

"But now I guess . . . this school is pretty cool. It takes some getting used to, but the school plays are awesome, and there are a bunch of cool kids here. There aren't really all those cliques you find at other schools, at least not in the same way. It's different here—people kinda just accept you for who you are. I guess what I'm trying to say is I don't want to go back to Oaks Crossing anymore. I like it here. Please don't get him fired."

So just like that she changes her mind. See what I mean? Dangerous with a capital D.

"So you're pretty sure then that your dad actually is clean?"

"Definitely," she said. "All he ever talks about is how much he loves it here. He said the kids are like none he's ever met before. He said he didn't know such a diverse school could even exist in today's world, whatever that means. And he just loves you, Mac! I mean, you should have heard the way he talked at the dinner table about what great ballplayers you and Vince are. He just raved about you guys."

I think she was kind of embarrassed to be telling me this, because she was looking at something behind me now and not saying that right to my face. That was okay;

I was pretty embarrassed myself. And it felt pretty awesome to know that Kjelson thought I was a good catcher.

"Well, then who's behind trying to get the school closed down?" I asked.

Hannah shrugged and then said, "Look, I gotta go, okay? And I expect a refund of my twenty dollars at some point."

I wanted to argue that point with her since she'd already caused me way more than twenty dollars' worth of headaches with all of her lies, but she trotted away, and I had enough on my mind right now anyway.

I waved Vince and Joe over. As they walked toward me, I realized that maybe there was some hope after all. If Kjelson wasn't behind this, the signs still pointed at him being involved somehow. That phone call we'd overheard in George's office had to mean something. So maybe Kjelson could at least provide us with a lead of some sort. Or maybe he would even help us, if he loved the school as much as Hannah claimed.

I filled Vince and Joe in on everything I'd just found out. They were about as shocked as I was.

"Well, we should go pay Mr. K. a visit, then," Vince said. "Maybe all that stuff you found in George's office means that he's been doing the same thing we have— trying to figure out where things went wrong. Maybe he was merely investigating things himself?"

Monday—Mr. Kjelson's Classroom

After school that day we found Mr. Kjelson at his desk working on something.

"Oh, come on in, guys," he said to us. "What's up?"

Vince and I looked at each other and we both made a silent agreement in that one quick look. It was time to come clean; more lies in this situation wouldn't lead us anywhere. The only way to get anywhere with Kjelson was going to be to tell him everything.

So we did.

We confessed it all. That we'd found out about a lot of weird things happening at the school and that we were convinced someone was trying to get it closed down. How we'd thought it might be him and about what we'd found in Dr. George's office backing up those beliefs. I didn't leave out the part about how I'd cheated on the SMARTs for the whole school that evening he saw us in the halls. I had to trust him all the way or nothing. Besides, that was what we still didn't get: if I'd cheated for everyone, then how had we all failed?

Mr. Kjelson looked pretty disappointed in us, and I didn't blame him. Here he'd thought we were good kids and now he was finding out that we'd cheated on a state test—not just for ourselves, but for every kid in the school.

"Boys, I'm glad you're coming clean, but this is unacceptable. I can't believe you guys would risk your futures like this."

All I could do was look at my shoes. I couldn't even stand to look at him. I felt so bad.

"But," he continued, "I have to admit I can see why you did it. And that your hearts were in the right place. Because I agree, I've been suspecting the same thing you have. And it's just as bad as you feared, too. The meeting that's happening on Tuesday is going to be over whether to close this school down immediately. And I have to admit, it seems like it's going to happen at this point."

"I'm so sorry. I just thought I was the one guy who could save the school," I said.

Mr. Kjelson actually laughed, but it was pretty humorless. He killed it off with a sigh. "The part I still don't get is who is behind all of this? Who would go to such lengths to shut this place down and why?"

"*Maybe*," Vince said, "the person actually responsible for the recent events is the drama teacher, Louie-Booey, and he is actually the leader of an alien race of peoples who worship chocolate pudding, broken tennis rackets, and hairless dogs. And the changes in the school are merely intended to help make the place more habitable for their eventual invasion and takeover because their home planet was filled with failure and small animal poop, and they needed deep-fried, fatty foods to survive. Really, with the way things have been going lately, this one almost seems like the most reasonable option to me at this point."

Kjelson and I laughed out loud at that one in spite of the overall gloomy mood. That was why I loved Vince: he could always bring out the laughter in even the worst situations.

"But seriously, why are you the only teacher who seems to care?" Vince asked. "And I still don't get how one test can have this kind of impact."

"Well, most of the other teachers either thought I was a crazy conspiracy theorist or were scared for their careers," Mr. Kjelson said. "It seems someone has been threatening them. And well, sadly there are a few who just don't seem to care at all."

Mr. Kjelson then explained to us about this new legislation that required a certain percentage of the school's students to meet minimum standards. If a school did not meet those bare minimum test scores, then there was an emergency provision that could call for immediate closure of that school. But the test scores would have to be universally, ridiculously low for that to happen. A school full of chimpanzees could probably meet those minimum standards. Yet unfortunately our students had not. Whoever had altered the tests after us saw to that.

"Isn't there anything we can do?" I asked.

"I'm afraid it may be too late. That meeting is Tuesday. They think it's imperative that this place be shut down pretty quickly."

"But they can't just, I mean . . ."

"I'm sorry, but I'm afraid they can. It's been done successfully before in other states and school districts and it'll happen again. Usually it's for other reasons, but I don't think this will be unheard of. Whoever staged all this did a good job. I mean, there are health code violations, the lunch menu was blatantly negligent for a time, gym fitness standards aren't being met, there are bully problems, and as far as government officials, local school district officials, and state education administrators can tell, our students failed the SMARTs in record numbers. From the outside this school looks like a disaster right now, even with all the good work Dr. George has done to try and clean it up.

"But that still leads us back to who and why," Kjelson said again. I could tell that he hated mysteries as much as I did, especially ones that involved him losing his job. "What could anyone possibly have to gain from this school being shut down? It makes no sense."

"Actually, it makes perfect sense," said a voice from the doorway. "There's plenty to gain from it."

The office was silent for a long time as we all stared at the newcomer. I think we were all in shock.

Dr. George entered the room and closed the door behind him.

"And you haven't even heard the best part yet," he said with a gut-wrenching and utterly sick, crooked smile on his cracked face.

Chapter 25

Monday—Mr. Kjelson's Classroom

"It was you?" Mr. Kjelson said. Practically shouted, actually.

Dr. George just smiled at first as he approached us. I was so confused now that I thought I might pass out. Which probably would have been pretty funny in any other situation. This made even less sense than ever now. I'd known the Suits were bad, but I'd never imagined just how evil they actually were.

"It was me," he said with that horrible, horrible smile still on his face.

"But why?" I said.

"Because this school is corrupted!" he nearly shouted. "It's you, and kids like you. You're vermin. All you do is run around and cause trouble. You don't show any respect for the teachers or your elders; you don't pay attention in class; you interfere with the real students getting the education they deserve. You're like a virus, a drain on the system.

"So I'm fixing it. After this place's miserable failure, the city school board and district officials will be ripe for a solution. They'll be willing to try anything, you see? I'll give them my presentation, my proposal for a new charter school, publicly funded, privately run, where I can make sure rules are enforced like they're meant to be. You think this is my first trip to the rodeo? I've been doing this for years.

"Our institution will be one of real higher education. It will be *American*. With the right teachers who demand respect. We're bringing the all-American educational system back to the all-American boys and girls. So they can succeed, like they were born to. You probably don't get that, do you? You don't understand any of this. You were born to fail. But now you won't get to spread your rule-breaking disease to the good kids. Not anymore. I don't know how that old fool Dickerson let your crap go on for so long," he sneered. "You are the sort of filth that has ruined our school system!"

"How did you do all this stuff before you even worked here?" Kjelson asked.

"I have my connections. School board members, cafeteria workers, other teachers. Everybody has their price, especially in the education system, where salaries are laughably low. Do you know what it's like for these teachers to work so much harder than the teacher down the hall but yet get paid exactly the same? Well, it ruins them. Besides, getting menus altered, coaching changes, leaving poop all over the school, all that stuff is easy. It's doctoring standardized tests like the SMARTs that's the hard part. But that's the only part that really matters. All the other things were just window dressing to make me look good while I was tearing this place down. So I made sure I was brought in before the SMARTs were administered. Then I made sure everyone failed them.

"And this is where I get to the best part," he said, his smile growing. "You'll especially love this, *Mac*. I didn't even do anything to the SMARTs. You did. You were the one who rigged the test and caused everyone to fail."

He looked right at me as I stood there and shook my head, refusing to believe what he was saying to me. There was no way. No, I'd corrected the tests, not the other way around. It wasn't possible.

It was like he could read my mind. "No? You don't believe me?" he asked. "Well, you should. Because I planted fake answer sheets in my office. You see, I knew you'd try to cheat. You're a troublemaker through and through. You don't do what I've been doing as long as I have without getting to know your type, Christian. As soon as I met you, I knew I was on to something. I knew about your business, and I used it to my advantage, to make it so the school would fail the test and my hands would be perfectly clean. You see, you think I didn't have a way to get into your silly little office before I had the locks changed? That the vice principal couldn't get a key to a bathroom in his own school? That's just you being a fool, Mac.

"I've always had access to your office, to your little notebooks. So I knew about your plan to cheat on the tests. All I had to do was count on you to be you, trying to be a big shot and solve everyone's problems. I planted those fake answer keys, trusting you to cheat. And guess what? It worked! It was all you—you are the reason that all of these teachers will lose their jobs, that all of these kids will lose their school. I'm much obliged, Mac. Now all the kids will benefit from a proper education at my new charter school. All the ones we decide to let in, anyways."

I opened and closed my mouth, but I couldn't speak. I didn't think I was even breathing anymore.

"That's just sick, Dr. George," Mr. Kjelson said softly.

Dr. George laughed in response.

"Why? Because all I did was count on this little

rule-breaker to break the rules like he has been doing his whole life? I'm not the sick one here; he is. Also, I know you broke in and got all your stuff back. You won't be expelled. Your permanent record will be fine. But it doesn't matter anymore. The scores are in. The school's going to get shut down, and there's nothing the three of you can do about it. Have a nice life, guys."

Dr. George turned and left, laughing. And he was right. It was all over, and it was entirely my fault.

After he left, the room was silent for a long time. I was left with my thoughts, which I didn't want to think about.

All I had been trying to do was solve kids' problems, and I hadn't thought about the consequences, about the damage that could be done by school-wide cheating. But that wasn't true either. . . . I had been thinking more about the money than helping everybody. I hated to admit it to myself, but it was the truth. The thought of making over a thousand dollars on one job had blinded me from the possible disaster of trying to cheat on a test on such a massive scale.

Sure, George had shut down an entire school all to get back at a few kids who caused problems. Basically for money and so he could do things his own way. And now it seemed obvious to me: I'd done some pretty extreme things for money myself. Were we really all that different? The biggest reason I had been upset was because I'd lose my business. I may have helped kids as I was making money off them. And I would have never accepted a job that hurt innocent people. But that was a lie, because I'd done just that. Maybe not on purpose, exactly, but the end result was the same either way.

And the worst part of all was that George was right: there was nothing we could do. We had no proof that he was behind all of this. It was our word against his. All we could do now was sit and watch the school close down. I was going to get a front-row seat to watch my actions destroy the lives of all of these awesome teachers and kids.

And that was when I realized what my selfishness had been blinding me from this whole time. Since I'd heard about the SMART scores and George had stolen everything from my office, I'd really only been worried about myself, about what would happen to *me* if the school closed down, instead of thinking about the school itself. This school was one of a kind. It deserved better than me. But maybe if, for once, I finally put the school and all of the kids here ahead of myself, we still had a chance. It was time I started doing this like a real old-school baseball player would. I needed to play for the team and not for the stats.

"So that's it, then?" Vince finally said.

Kjelson didn't say anything; he just looked at the floor.

But I did. I said, "No."

They both looked at me, startled.

"I'm finished here; that much is clear. My business can be no more. But this doesn't have to be the end for everyone else. Dr. George was counting on me to keep acting like the selfish kid that I am. He assumed I'd only still be thinking about saving myself, about what's best for me. But that's where his plan has a weakness."

I had Vince's and Kjelson's full attention now.

"I'm turning myself in to the higher-up Suits. I have the evidence that proves it was me who fixed the tests so that we all failed. If I turn that in, then maybe they'll agree to readminister the tests. If they know that one kid caused our school to fail, then maybe they'll give everyone else another chance. George said it himself: all that other stuff like the rodent poop and school lunches, that stuff is just extra; the tests are what really matter. And we have evidence in my Books and on my DVR discs that I was responsible for the failure. I'll probably get expelled, but that's okay; I deserve it. At least the school would get to stay open. Besides, if my business can cause this kind of damage, then the school is probably better off without it anyway."

"Mac, you can't do this. You're not the only one at fault here," Vince said.

"Yes I am. Without me there'd be no business. There's no point in anybody taking the fall but me."

"No, there's no way I'm letting you take the fall alone. I don't care if it means I won't make the baseball team or get expelled myself. I'm in this, too. You always say this is our business not just yours, and you can't take that back now."

I nodded. Vince really was my best friend, and if I was going to ruin my life to save the school and he wanted to be there with me, then I wasn't going to argue. Because there's no one else I'd rather have with me at a moment like that.

"I'm proud of what you're willing to do here, Christian," Mr. Kjelson said. "I'll help as much as I can to make sure you're heard."

Chapter 26

Tuesday—The Olson Olson Theatre

It might seem weird to risk further punishment by sneaking out of the house to go to a school meeting when you're grounded. But sneaking out tonight was easy because my parents weren't home. They were at the same meeting I was attending, along with probably over half the neighborhood.

Vince met up with me at my place, and then we went there together. Students weren't normally allowed to attend open school board meetings, but tonight's was different since it was so important.

"Are you ready?" Mr. Kjelson asked as we met up with him near the back entrance of the theater.

I nodded. "I'm going to do what I have to do to save the school," I said.

Mr. Kjelson nodded solemnly.

We sat next to him near the back of the theater. Right now there were several guys in suits sitting in chairs on the stage, including both Principal Dickerson and Vice Principal George. The other three guys I did not recognize. I figured they were probably the principals' bosses.

The crowd was pretty loud as all the parents and kids in attendance anxiously and openly debated what might be the outcome of the meeting. I waited patiently as some lady who I figured was some kid's mom began talking through a microphone about the meeting agenda. I kept my eyes on the cracked face of Dr. George and his stiff, fake hair.

After a few minutes she introduced some guy in a suit named Mr. Simpson. He got to the podium and announced that the school had been having issues lately, including astoundingly poor state standardized test scores, health code problems, and nutritional violations with school lunches, and that in light of those issues, the school board had decided that the school was going to have to be closed immediately as an unfit environment for learning.

The crowd basically exploded like a parade taking

place on a minefield during an earthquake. People shouted questions out of turn. Guys were standing and shaking their fists in outrage, as if that would solve anything. I saw many people crying. I thought I even saw one older lady faint.

Mr. Simpson tried to calm the crowd. "Now listen, this was not an easy decision, but we've determined that the issues facing this school cannot be easily fixed. Definitely not within this school year. This is for the best in terms of your children's educations."

"What issues? These SMART test things are worthless; they're complete . . ." some guy started yelling before his wife shushed him.

"Your questions are valid. I'm going to bring Vice Principal George to the mike to answer them for you. But please, let's try to keep this orderly and civil," Mr. Simpson said before stepping aside.

Dr. George got up and moved to the podium. He leaned into the microphone and cleared his throat.

"I know you're all upset," he said in his typically curt and blunt manner, without even saying good evening or anything like that. "I will do my best to answer your questions and explain the reasons for our actions. Now, you, sir, you can go first."

He pointed at a guy up front who had his hand raised.

"How do we know these tests weren't bogus? I mean,

my kid, he is a smart kid. He, like, just wouldn't do this badly, you know?"

Dr. George nodded and then started shaking his head abruptly. "I assure you all that the validity of these tests has not been compromised. They are strictly regulated and carefully monitored. There's just no way. Additionally, there's . . ."

That's when Kjelson tapped my leg, and we made our move. Vince, Kjelson, and I stood and walked toward the stage. Dr. George saw us coming and stopped in the middle of whatever phony, canned answer he'd been giving to the angry parent. The whole theater hushed as we walked up on stage.

"You can't be up here," Dr. George finally said to us.

"I'm Mr. Kjelson, a teacher here and a parent, and I have some very interesting information to present regarding this whole mess!" Mr. Kjelson shouted. "If you'll hear me?"

The crowd applauded. It was unenthusiastic, but Mr. Kjelson was given the stage. He stepped to the microphone and introduced Vince and me as students here who had something they wanted to confess.

"What we're about to say to you may be pretty shocking," Kjelson said. "But you'll hear for yourself." He turned to me and handed me the microphone.

I faced the crowd. The microphone hit my chin a few

times because my hand was shaking so hard. I couldn't believe I was about to publicly out my whole business to the school and my parents. But it had to be done. I knew that, and the more I thought about saving the school, the less nervous I became.

"Hi," I said into the microphone. My voice sounded so loud through the PA system that it startled me. "You probably don't know me, but my name is Christian Barrett. I run a business here at the school. I solve problems. And it was my fault that everyone failed the SMARTs. I cheated. I cheated for everybody, that is. Vince and I, we broke into the school and altered everybody's answers."

There was a wave of gasps and then dead silence. I took that as my cue to continue.

"The thing is, I was only trying to help. I'd heard how important the tests were, and I didn't want the school to get closed down. So I stole what I thought were the answer keys and tried to make sure everyone would pass. I thought I was helping everybody, helping the school. I never wanted this to happen. But I know it was a mistake, that I screwed up. I have proof, too."

Mr. Kjelson walked over and handed the three Suits onstage a bag containing my Books and DVR discs: the ones that showed us sitting in the fourth stall making our plan to cheat on the SMARTs.

"In those notebooks and on those discs you'll find plenty of evidence that backs up my claim. So, you see, the kids didn't fail. I caused them to, accidentally."

The three Suits immediately started conferring with one another; Dickerson joined them. The audience erupted in gasps and murmurs. I couldn't look at them, for fear of seeing my parents' faces.

One parent shouted, "The tests need to be retaken!" and there were a few halfhearted claps in support of this idea. But most of the people there still seemed to be trying to get over the initial shock.

Then Mr. Simpson stepped forward and held out his hand. I gave him the microphone. He gave me a look that would have melted my brains if I hadn't ducked just slightly.

Mr. Simpson tapped on the microphone and it squealed loudly. The loud whine quieted the crowd just enough for him to be heard.

"Clearly, in light of recent events, we will be delaying our decision regarding this school indefinitely, pending an investigation. The evidence presented will be thoroughly reviewed, and if the integrity of the test is found to have been compromised, then steps will be taken for the readministering of the tests to the school. And in light of these doubts surrounding the SMARTs, some discussion will need to be had over possibly not administering them this year at all. In the meantime school will continue here at Thomas Edison at least through the remainder of the school year to give us the appropriate time to conduct a full investigation."

The kids in attendance all cheered, and the parents seemed pretty happy, too. Now, probably not all kids were going to be so happy, because there are some kids who just hate school no matter what, but our school was pretty unique. Likely how the kids here were acting was how most of the students would feel when the news would break the next day.

I glanced at Dr. George. His face was red and he was almost vibrating with anger. He was doing his best to keep it all in, though, I could tell, because publicly his goal was to save the school. And he didn't want to blow his cover since there still wasn't anything that would tie him to all of this. But, man, was he mad. He was shooting blazing fireballs at me out of his eyes. To be honest, seeing that kinda made confessing worth it.

Vince and I stepped down from the stage, and I finally went over to where my parents were sitting. They looked shocked. And angry. And they should have been both. I knew that my business was definitely over now, and part of me almost felt relieved. Having that business had been a lot of stress. It had been quite a huge thing to keep secret from every adult around me, so it almost felt good to finally be done sneaking around.

My dad glared at me. "We're so disappointed in you," he said.

"I can't believe you boys would do this," my mom said. She looked destroyed.

"That said," my dad continued, "I'm very proud that you did the right thing in the end. That took a lot of guts, to own up to your mistakes."

I nodded, but he still hadn't stopped giving me the old dagger eyes.

That's when I saw George headed our way. I nudged Vince, and then we glanced at each other. This couldn't be good.

He smiled as he approached, one of his patented shark-on-rollerblades, awkward smiles. His attempts at smiling just split his face in half like cracked, dry wood. I didn't like this one bit.

"Hi, Mr. and Mrs. Barrett," he said. I'd never, ever heard him sound this friendly.

"Hi," my dad said, shaking his hand.

"Can I have a word with these two? I want to commend them for coming forward and doing the right thing," Dr. George said.

My mom smiled and nodded. "I don't see why not."

"It's a little loud in here. Why don't we step outside?" he said to us.

Vince and I followed him out of the theater. On our way out I saw Hannah sitting in the production booth in the back of the theater. Our eyes locked. I tried to apologize in that one look, but I could see I didn't have to. She smiled at me, and I smiled back.

Then we were out in the empty hallway. Just me, Vince, and Dr. George. Of course I was terrified. I knew how mad he was; I'd just ruined everything for him. What was he going to do?

He grabbed the back of our necks just then. Not too hard but firm enough to tell us that we'd better let him take us wherever he had in mind.

"This way," he said.

He led us toward the East Wing. Toward my old office. Along the way no one talked. I was too terrified to say anything, and I think George was probably too angry. I had no idea about Vince, but he always has been pretty bad at any confrontations, except for those that occur between pitcher and batter, so he probably just didn't even know what to say at all.

We got to the East Wing boys' bathroom, and Dr. George unlocked the door. Then he held it open and said, "After you."

We shuffled inside.

That's when he exploded.

"You little . . ." Well, I'm not going to repeat

everything he said, but I'll just say that his face bulged, and he screamed at us and called us names for several minutes before calming himself enough to have a somewhat normal conversation.

"You ruined everything!" he yelled. "I had this all planned so perfectly, and you screwed it all up. Do you have any idea how many strings I had to pull, how hard it was to get all of this set up? To stage all of this to where it could look like I was doing such a great job cleaning up the school and to set you up to rig the SMARTs? And now it's all ruined.

"Mark my words, you will pay for this. They don't call me Dr. Discipline over in Harrison School District for nothing. At that high school I got no fewer than ten kids sent to juvie! And that's where you're both going. I have my connections in there, too. So just you wait. Your life will be a living hell. And you'll deserve it."

Vince and I looked at each other. We didn't know what to say. I knew there was nothing I could do to stop him. And besides, he was probably right: I probably did deserve it for all of the years my business had benefited from other kids' misfortunes.

"Well? What do you have to say now, *Mac*? What about you, Vincent? Huh?"

Vince cleared his throat. "Well, sir, I'd like to quote my grandma if I can?"

"What?" Dr. George sneered.

I smirked. Even in this dire situation I couldn't help it. There was no one I'd rather meet this with head-on than this guy. Vince was the best. It was that simple.

"Well, if she were here right now, she'd probably say, 'Be careful what you wish for because for every wish there's a demented magical unicorn out there looking to impale someone right in their face.' "

"What!" Dr. George shouted. "That's sick, you little . . ."

It was pretty sick, I had to admit. But she really did say that. I'd heard her say it once at a funeral for one of her friends, right when the pastor was going through a prayer. It was pretty funny in a totally sick way, of course.

Anyway, Dr. George didn't get to finish his sentence because just then the door burst open and Mr. Simpson, Mr. Dickerson, the other two Suits, Mr. Kjelson, and several parents all rushed inside. From the looks on their faces I could tell something was up.

"Dr. George," Mr. Simpson said. "Perhaps you should step outside with us?"

"Why? What's going on?" he demanded.

Mr. Kjelson pointed up in the corner where our camera was still mounted. "Everything that has been happening in here just played on the big screen in the Olson Olson Theatre."

"What? No, that's not possible. The recorders aren't even in here!" Dr. George yelled.

"It's a wireless signal," Hannah said from the doorway. "Anything can pick it up; it doesn't just have to be those DVRs."

I hadn't noticed her arrival until just then. I made a mental note that I would need to thank her in a big way, since she had just saved us, basically.

Dr. George shook his head.

You had to love that. In the end he was taken down by his own old-man ignorance of technology. Okay, that probably isn't fair to say, but he deserves it. What I didn't know was how Hannah had known to play the signal in the theater and how anyone had known we were in here.

"Let's go, Dr. George," Mr. Simpson said again calmly. "I think it's best if we all step outside."

For the first time all night nobody spoke. Dr. George stood there with his ancient word hole hanging wide open, shaking his head from side to side as if he was trying to tell people that that wasn't really him. Then he rubbed his eyes and shuffled outside with Dickerson and the three Suits. The parents followed.

I found my mom and dad as we all left the building, and my mom hugged Vince and me. I don't think they had forgotten how angry they were with me; they were probably just happy that it was all over with. I didn't say much. It had been a tiring night, and I was sure the next day would be worse whenever we found out what our punishment would be.

Then when we got to the car, I saw someone wave at me from behind the portables. I wasn't sure who it was exactly, but I had an idea.

"Hey, Vince and I rode our bikes here, so shouldn't we ride them back?"

My dad pondered this. "Yeah, I suppose. But come right home."

I nodded. Then they got into the car and drove off. I motioned for Vince to follow me over to the portables.

Chapter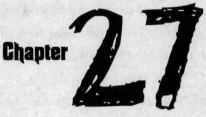

Tuesday—The Portables

Around back we ran into the person who had waved at me.

"So you tapped into the camera's wireless signal and played that in the theater?"

Hannah grinned at me. "Yeah. AV club came in handy after all, huh? Anyway, it's gonna cost you."

I laughed even though I knew she probably wasn't kidding. I took out some money and handed it to her. I always kept a decent amount of money on me—it was good business practice. But I supposed that was something I was going to have to get over now that my business was finished.

"I do owe you," I said. "How did you know to do that?"

"I saw you guys heading off toward the bathroom with Dr. George and knew something must be up. So I ran back to the theater and found the wireless signal coming off those cameras. Doing the rest was easy; it's what I do," she said as she took off her mittens to put the money into her pocket.

"Well, thanks," I said.

"So I guess your business is kaput?" Hannah asked.

I nodded.

"Well, hey, I think it's cool what you both did to save the school. I mean, it was your fault in the first place, but I think it was a really great thing to give up your business for the rest of us."

"Thanks," I said again, trying not to blush. It was a pretty cold night, so likely my cheeks were too red for her to tell anyway.

"So now what?" Vince said.

"Now I just want to thank you guys for buying me a new iPhone," Hannah said, and then laughed while patting the money she'd just put in her pocket.

"Me. You mean, thank *me*, right?" I said. "After all, it was *my* money."

"Whatever, Mac. This business was just as much mine as it was yours! We both bought her a new phone!" Vince said.

"Vince, come on, admit it already. You're, like, obsessed

with Hannah or something. It's kind of pathetic."

"Me?" he screeched. I'd never seen Vince this animated before. "You're the one who has been, like, going to the ends of the Earth to keep me away from her because you know she likes me better. I make her laugh more and you're jealous. You're jealous because you get all, like, nervous and stupid around her but I make her laugh!"

"Jerk!" I yelled. "That's not . . ."

I stopped when I realized that Hannah was hysterical. She was basically on the ground rolling in the almost frozen dirt, she was laughing so hard. Vince and I both stopped and watched as she straightened herself and wiped at her eyes. She was actually crying.

"Did you guys forget I was standing right here?" she said as the echoes of her last laughs died away.

Vince and I looked at each other. Neither of us spoke.

"Seriously, you guys are so hilariously cute. I'd love to stand around all night and watch you go at it like a couple of bickering old ladies, but I think I'd end up dying from laughing so much. Honestly, though, you guys are adorable, but you need to stop fighting. You'll find yourselves a couple of cute girls someday, I promise. Anyways, I gotta go. Maybe I'll see you around sometime."

Hannah waved and then walked away. Vince and I stood side by side and watched her go. I wondered if he felt as stupid as I did. I was afraid to even look at him.

We stood there awhile not saying anything, not even looking at each other.

Then I broke the awkward silence. "So who was the last Cub pitcher to win twenty games?"

He didn't say anything. He just glared at me, and I couldn't tell what he was thinking. Then finally after what seemed like forever, he spoke.

"That would be the 'great' slider specialist Jon Leiber in 2001, who went twenty and six."

I couldn't help but laugh. It was so weird. I'd been kind of mad at him just a few minutes before, but suddenly it was all gone.

"I thought I'd stumped you," I said, turning to face him.

He grinned and said, "You? Stump me? Ha-ha. Ha-ha-ha-ha!"

"Whatever. It could happen," I said as we started walking toward where we'd stashed our bikes earlier.

"Yeah, maybe if I let my grandma perform brain surgery on me. *Maybe* then, but I still doubt it."

I nodded. "Yeah, you're probably right. I think your Grandma is crazy like crazy genius or whatever. She'd probably upgrade your brain to give you telekinetic powers or something. That's all we'd need: a Vince who can move stuff with his brain."

"No, I'd probably use my powers to somehow get the Cubs into the World Series."

I nodded solemnly at this. There was no joking when it came to the Cubs and the World Series. It mattered that much.

"Speaking of," Vince said, "now that I've answered your unbelievably simple Cubs question, I have one that I've been saving up for a special occasion. One that you'll never get right. Not in a million years. Not even if I let my grandma perform surgical upgrades on *your* brain instead. Not even if I transplanted Joe Blanton's brain into your head and then injected it with, like, Jayson Stark's brain cells. Not even if you *owned* the Cubs. Not even if I told you the answer right after asking the question. It's that hard. Your brain won't even be able to comprehend the complex nature of the question and its answer. You wouldn't even get it right if—"

"Vince," I said laughing. "I get the point. Just hit me with it already."

Epilogue

So maybe you're wondering how everything played out. And well, I'd be lying if I said everything simply continued on as normal. But the great news was that we actually didn't get expelled. I don't know how, exactly. Perhaps it had something to do with the fact that we were threatened in a bathroom by a school employee, and we had video evidence and witnesses to prove it. But whatever the reason, we were relieved to still be in school.

Still, there was a price to be paid. Vince and I were both declared ineligible to play baseball that year, which stunk, of course. We also each got suspended for two weeks. Forgive me here for being honest, but I didn't see how in the world they considered suspension a punishment. I mean, basically, Vince and I got ten free days off from school in which we sat around and played video games and talked about the Cubs. It was freaking awesome! Seriously, if that's what happens when you get caught with a business like mine, then I wished I would have gotten caught years ago.

Except that wasn't entirely true because we also got a community service project to work on. Turns out, that was a pretty good punishment. Because who likes to walk around all day picking up trash? Sure, we were helping to keep the earth clean and blah, blah, blah, but that still didn't make it fun. That said, I'd much rather have had to do that for the next eight weekends than to be kicked out of school. Plus, they let Vince and I serve our time together, which was pretty cool, because then we basically just made fun of Joe Blanton and challenged each other with Cubs trivia while picking up garbage all day.

Anyways, after the suspension I bet you're thinking there was some way that I got my business back, right? Well, nope. I didn't. My business was finished. I'd outed myself in front of Dickerson; there was no coming back from that. So we shut down the business completely. And that was okay, actually. It was kind of nice to just be a normal kid and only have to worry about going to school and playing video games and watching the Cubs screw up another perfectly good off-season by trading for washed-up old players and signing second-rate garbage instead of the real superstars who were on the free-agent market.

Old Georgie eventually got arrested and charged for something or other. I wasn't sure what exactly, since I didn't speak Nerdy Lawyer talk, but I got the impression it was pretty serious. He even got sentenced to some prison time. And the SMARTs were also disbanded as official state tests, since George had helped to create them.

So school went on as usual for everybody else. The plays continued, with Louie-Booey dazzling everybody with his hilarious scripts and giving the kids the freedom to make the plays their own. And our school sports teams continued to dominate. Mr. Kjelson did a great job with our baseball team. They were 6–1 after our first seven games. It was tough to watch them from the stands, but Vince and I were both sure we'd be out there next year as seventh graders.

It took a while to get used to life without my business. After all, I'd had it since I was in second grade.

But just when I thought I was out . . . they pull me back in.

It was a day like any other day. I was walking home from school, starting to appreciate how simple life can be for kids without complicated and powerful businesses in organized crime to run. Vince had had to leave school early to watch his baby sister while his mom was at work, so I was alone. And I heard someone walk up behind me.

"Hey, Christian. I mean, *Mac*. Look, I need your help."

I didn't turn around. I simply said, "I'm sorry. You're too late. I'm not in that line of work anymore."

"I think you'll make an exception for me."

I suddenly realized how familiar that voice sounded. I'd always sworn I'd never forget it. I turned around slowly to see if it really could be true.

It took a few seconds for my eyes to adjust to the bright sun. He was just a silhouette at first, but then he stepped closer and it all came rushing back.

"I need your help, Mac," Staples said, his smile as wide and as dangerous as it ever was. It still looked like he had more teeth than any human being needed. "Please?"

Acknowledgments

Thanks to Chris Richman for invaluable feedback and always being willing to argue the finer points of Joe Blanton's astonishing life and career. Thanks to Mom, Dad, Mike, Kayla, Nic, Jes, Schuylar, Ashley, John, Sharon, and all of my family and friends for their continued support. Thanks to Debbie Kovacs and everyone at Walden Media and HarperCollins. Thanks to Kellie Celia for working so hard on my behalf. Thanks to my fantastic editor, Jordan Brown, for always defending Derek Jeter as if he was his own brother even though deep down he knows he's wrong. Thanks to my agent, Steven Malk, for introducing me to children's literature, and for taking my panicked 4:00 a.m. phone calls when someone offers me a trade in fantasy baseball and I need advice. Thanks to all of the kids, parents, teachers, librarians, and walruses who have emailed me—getting those messages is my favorite part about being an author. Also important were my pockets, because they hold stuff for me, and my shoes, because they protect my awesome feet. Thank you to run-on sentences, I need you. Finally, thank you again to my best friend and beautiful wife, Amanda, for always supporting and encouraging me.

Staples is back?
How could that be?
Turn the page
for a sneak peek at

The Fourth Stall
PART III

Staples still looked like Staples in that he still looked like he'd just gotten back from eating a nice leisurely lunch that had consisted of sick kids' puppies. But he also looked pretty different in some ways, too. For instance, instead of a shaved head, Staples now had short dark hair that was neatly combed. And instead of his usual tank top or T-shirt, he was wearing an untucked dress shirt and a skinny necktie and dark jeans. He looked like any other normal kid. Well, except for the evil smile and the dark eyes so black that even nighttime was afraid of them, that is.

In case you're not aware of who Staples is, which is unlikely considering he is a legend around these parts, he used to run a business kind of like mine. The only difference was that his business was dirty. He fixed things in his favor and rarely ever showed kids mercy. He'd beat you to death with your own arm if it somehow benefited him. And last year I'd gotten involved in an all-out war against him and his cronies. In the end, with help from my friends, we'd managed to take down his whole empire. Not long after that, we got word that he'd skipped town. And I had truly believed I would never see him again.

But I had been wrong.

Standing there now inside his impossibly large shadow, I tried to stand my ground. That's what I've learned about predators from the Discovery channel since my first run-in with Staples: Don't ever show your fear. Predators prey on the weak.

But he could see right through it, of course.

"Relax, Mac," he said. "If I was here to get revenge, you'd already be bleeding."

I managed to blurt out an awkward chuckle that only made Staples smile wider.

"And besides, I don't really want to get any of your blood on my shirt."

I took a deep breath and used every ounce of seventh grader I had to finally say something.

"So . . . what, um, do you want, then?"

Great job of not sounding weak and afraid.

"Well, I'm trying to turn my life around. 'Fly straight,' as my nerdy counselor likes to say," Staples said.

"Counselor?"

"Yeah, I've got this court-appointed counselor I go see once a week. You know, to help get me on my feet. I am eighteen with no legal guardian anymore, you know. I have to take care of myself."

"Court-appointed?" I asked lamely, not knowing what else to say.

"Yeah, I did a stint in juvie shortly after our, uh, *run-in* last year. Part of the deal my lawyer copped with the judge for me was that upon my release I'd have to start seeing this counselor. You know, to help make sure I don't ever find my way into real prison. But I don't even need him for that. I realized the error of my ways on my own."

I really had no idea what to say to this so I merely nodded. I thought if I even tried to speak I might accidentally yell, "Liar!" And then kick him in the shin and run. But that probably wouldn't play out to my advantage in the end, so I stayed quiet. Which was fine because Staples just kept talking.

"Yeah, anyway, he's a real dork, my counselor. But I guess he's trying to help me or whatever, so I try to stomach him and his dumb motivational sayings. You know what he actually says to me basically every time I see him?"

I shook my head.

"He says, 'Barry, *perception is reality.*' Can you believe that? He even says it all profoundly just like that. Like it's the most genius thing anyone has ever said. How lame is that?"

I had absolutely no idea what Staples was talking about now, so I just nodded dumbly. *Perception is reality?* What did that even mean?

Staples was still Staples after all, so of course he could read me like a book. Which meant he saw right through my pretending to understand what he was talking about. He laughed at me.

"Mac, just trust me when I say that if anyone ever uses that phrase, they're either an idiot or a liar. Or both. Because reality is what is real. Intent and actions are real. Perception is just that: a different and individual awareness of the reality that exists; that's why there are two separate words for it. And don't even get me started on the quantum physics angle, because then that phrase has a totally different meaning altogether, scientifically speaking, and last time I checked, my counselor definitely wasn't a quantum physicist."

"Umm . . ."

Staples laughed at my embarrassingly obvious lack of

comprehension. I felt uncomfortable thinking about just how smart he might actually be. I had always known he was smart, but his ferocity and criminal intent had perhaps always hidden the true extent of his intelligence.

"So what exactly do you need help with?" I asked, anxious to get away from this new intellectual version of Staples. Somehow, seeing him act even remotely nice and civil made me more nervous than when he was just a flat-out psychopath.

"I was getting to that," he said. "So I'm still trying to get custody of my sister. Right now she's living with foster parents and, according to what I've seen and read, some foster kids grow up to be just like my dad: drug-addicted, jobless, hairy, and for some reason they also always seem to collect weird crap, like used paper plates or hippopotamus figurines or, in my dad's case, orange highlighters."

"That's great," I said. "Well, I mean the part about you trying to do something good, not that foster kids sometimes end up like your dad. But, anyways, what could I even do to help you?"

Staples furrowed his mean eyebrows.

"What gives, man? Isn't that supposed to be your *thing*?" he practically shouted.

It was the first real glimpse he'd shown of what I knew he really was deep down. And I took a step back, deciding whether or not to either book it now or see if I couldn't distract him somehow first and then make my getaway.

"Well, yeah, but no, I mean, not anymore. I told you, I'm retired."

Staples grabbed the front of his forehead like he had a headache. I could tell he was trying to stay under control. It dawned on me how close I probably was to getting my left eye punched out the back of my head by this monster.

"Besides," I added quickly, "she doesn't even go to my school, does she? I mean, I kind of specialized in stuff at my school itself."

"No, she doesn't go to your school," he said flatly. "But I didn't either, did I? Yet you still somehow managed that problem okay, didn't you?"

He had a point. And it was pretty awkward to stand there listening to him talk about how I had taken him down the year before. I'd crumbled his independent empire and now here I was saying that I wasn't really capable of doing such things.

"Well, that's kind of why I'm retired—every time I get involved, it only seems to make things worse. It always ends badly for *someone*."

"Didn't I hear that you just saved your school recently? That doesn't sound like it ended badly to me," Staples said. "Sounds like you won, as usual."

"It's not about 'winning,' Staples; it was about solving problems and making money. And I was creating more problems than I was solving at the end, and also spending more money than I was making. Besides, I'm kind of in the same boat as you: I need to keep my nose clean. The Suits are kind of watching me, you know?"

As I said this, I nodded my head toward a car that was parked just down the street from us. Staples turned and looked. The plain gray sedan that had been parked there since Staples and I had started talking suddenly pulled out and peeled past us and down the street before turning a corner and heading out of sight.

As the car had driven past, the gleam off Mr. Dickerson's bald head had shined like a sniper's scope reflecting the sunlight.

Staples gave me a look.

"Yeah," I agreed, "it's insane. He's been following me every day after school. I mean, they're really paranoid. But it's hard to blame them. I've found out the hard way that businesses like mine usually lead only to trouble in the end. That's why I'm out."

Staples looked like he was about to protest, but in the end he just nodded.

"Don't you remember what you said to me the last time we spoke?" he asked.

"Yeah, I offered to help you get back on your feet . . . but that was a year ago. Things have changed."

"I guess they have," he said, sounding defeated. "Well, I suppose there's no point in me even telling you what exactly I wanted help with then, even though it was something that would have been right up your alley."

I was surprised at how easily he was giving up. I mean, he really could have forced me to help him if he'd wanted to. And now that he was giving up, I was kind of curious as to what exactly he thought I could do to help out his situation with his sister. But I knew better: if I started asking questions, then that'd be it; I'd be sucked right back into the life I was trying to avoid.

"I really am sorry, Staples. But you saw Dickerson. . . . The Suits are on me like glue stuck to the teeth of a second grader right now."

Staples didn't say anything else. He just nodded and turned to leave. And then without looking back, just like that, my old nightmare was gone. And I was still in one piece, which was why it was weird that I suddenly felt so horrible, guilty almost.

I know I said before that me getting pulled back into the Business all started with the visit from Staples. So okay, I admit it. Maybe Staples didn't exactly pull me back into my business directly, at least not that day, but the whole incident should have been the first sign that something was off.

If I'd seen the warning lights right then, maybe I could have avoided some of the insanity that followed. Stuff like swimming pools full of blood, guts, and body parts, and crazy third-grade Japanese assassins with precise, near-deadly hit man skills. The sort of stuff that happens only in terrible made-for-TV movies on Disney starring whatever teen pop-star happens to be popular that month. If I'd known what was going to happen, maybe I would have stolen a car, swung by Vince's place, and gotten us both the heck out of town before it could.

But I hadn't seen Staples's visit as that kind of sign. So instead I just walked home.